WITNESS TO PASSION

A GUARDING HER BODY NOVEL

NAIMA
SIMONE

Entangled Publishing, LLC
2614 South Timberline Road
Suite 109
Fort Collins, CO 80525
Visit our website at www.entangledpublishing.com.

Ignite is an imprint of Entangled Publishing, LLC.

Edited by Tracy Montoya
Cover design by LJ Anderson
Cover art by Dollar Photo Club

Manufactured in the United States of America

First Edition June 2015

ignite

To Gary. 143.

Chapter One

"Happy birthday!"

Fallon Wayland snorted at her best friend, Addisyn Roarke's, exuberant greeting. "Birthdays suck ass," she said into her phone.

A sharp gasp came from behind her, and with a wince, Fallon peeked over her shoulder and met the disapproving glare of Betty White's angry twin sister. *Sorry*, Fallon mouthed with an apologetic smile and a shrug before turning around. And tried to pretend the woman's furious stare didn't burn the back of her neck like a sniper's scope.

God, could this line move any slower? She glanced down at her watch. 8:30. She had twenty minutes to buy coffee for herself, her boss, Carolyn Task, and Carolyn's ass-grabby son, Mitchell, and *then* traverse the Charles Street morning traffic to Caro's event-planning office.

Well, damn. Unfortunately, her red cape and blue tights were at the cleaners.

"You're in a real chipper mood," Addy drawled. "This is your *birthday*, Debbie Downer. Cheer up."

Fallon rolled her eyes, shifting one step forward in the line that moved at the speed of a molasses-covered snail. "What's the purpose of birthdays anyway? To commemorate the day a person was born, rejoice in another year of life, celebrate wisdom gained and lessons learned. Yada, yada, yada. Blah, blah, blah."

They were all the same, just varying in degrees of suckiness, broken promises, and disappointments. And while today, on her twenty-fifth, she might not have suffered anything more catastrophic than being late for work because of a coffee run and enduring an eat-shit-and-die glare from an octogenarian... Well, the day was still young.

"That is so cynical. Even for you," Addy complained.

"Cynical, huh. Well, let's see. On my sixth birthday, I expected a party with all my friends, a magician, clown, and a pony. Instead Mom brought home a new stepdad and a surprise trip to Paris—which, by the way, didn't include me." Fallon ticked off one finger. "On my tenth, all I got was a numb butt from sitting for hours on the living room window seat, waiting for Dad to come pick me up. Unfortunately, a business trip trumped my birthday. On my fifteenth, Mom took my puppy—Dad's gift—to the pound because it crapped on her precious Persian rug." She ticked off another finger. "And on my eighteenth, I lost my virginity."

"Riiight." Addy sighed. "Brandon Hyatt."

"Two *meh* minutes of my life I'll never see again." Fallon snorted. "His basement couch had more of a thrill than I did."

She'd never told Addy about the other reason she hated

her eighteenth birthday with a passion. Shane Roarke and that ill-fated birthday kiss. The kiss—and esteem-shattering rejection—that had sent her running to Brandon and his couch in the first place.

She made a sound between disgust and…disgust. Just the name of Addy's older brother caused her scalp to itch. And her heart to pound. And her belly to clench. But that was neither here nor there. With his black hair, turquoise eyes, and amazing body, Shane Roarke could tempt a nun into changing camps.

Unfortunately, he was more pious and righteous than any bride of Christ could ever hope to be.

"All right, I have to place this order." Fallon said, finally stepping up to the counter. "Thanks for the birthday call, but I have to go. I'm running late as it is."

"Fine, fine." Addy sighed. "But don't forget. After work, you, me, The Dive," she instructed, naming their favorite dive-bar hangout. "Cold beers and hot men. Am I the best-est best friend evah or what?"

"Uh-huh, the bestest. Now I gotta go for real. See you tonight."

A few moments later, she picked up her order and exited the bustling shop at a fast clip. Ten minutes to get to work now. She ground her teeth together. *Damn*. Carolyn, aka the Event Planning Nazi, didn't accept tardiness for any reason—even if that reason included her own order to pick up coffee before shadowing her office's doorstep.

Moments later, she unlocked the passenger door of her beloved FiFi, the diamond-blue BMW convertible that had been a college graduation present from her father three years earlier. She adored the little car. Though a few years old, FiFi was the only thing she'd kept besides the clothes on her back when she walked away from the pampered and stifling life that had defined her for twenty-three years. The luxurious brownstone, the healthy bank account, and unlimited credit cards—gone. But the BMW? Shoot...her mama didn't raise no fool.

Well, actually Chelsea Grace Wayland Jury Chancellor hadn't raised her at all. But still...

She bent over and slid the cardboard holder with the coffee cups on the front seat of the car, all the while trying not to imagine what her ass looked like hanging outside the open door. Once satisfied the drinks wouldn't spill, she straightened and closed the door. If God decided to actually bless her on her birthday, she mused, traffic would miraculously be clear, and she could make it to work with a couple of minutes to spare...

"Oh damn." She winced, her cell phone pinging, signaling a text. It was probably Carolyn demanding, *Where the hell are you?* She removed the phone from the outside pocket of her purse and glanced down at the screen.

Huh. Not a text, but a Twitter notification from her boyfriend Jared.

Smiling, she swept her thumb across the screen. She'd been seeing Jared Combs, a fun-loving, if flighty, bartender for six months. Their relationship was...nice. Light, easy, nothing deep. True, sometimes she felt like they had a weird ménage between her, him, and his drinking buddies going on. But, when she had to work late or on weekends, he didn't complain. Didn't demand she give up her career to entertain him. Did they have a grand passion? No. But she'd done the run-through-men-like-water thing years ago and had long since thrown that Been There Done That T-shirt out. Jared was predictable, uncomplicated, safe.

Yes, sure, he wasn't future husband material, as Addy often complained. But for Fallon, that was one of his selling points. A wedding, husband—those were Addy's dreams, not hers. After witnessing the natural disaster that had been her parents' marriage, she had absolutely no desire to walk down that aisle—literally. *Oh hell no*.

She stared down at Jared's tweet waiting in horrifying—mortifying—disbelief.

Sorry @Fallonwayland1. We're just not working out. I need a change & can't do that with u. Gotta do me. Need the keys to my apt back. Thanx.

What the *fuck*? Did he…? She squeezed her eyes shut, counted to ten. Reopened them. Nope, still there. This asshat had just broken up with her. By a Tweet. *A goddamn Tweet*. In 140 characters exactly. Really? He didn't even have the decency to private message her, but posted it for all of Twitterverse to see. Who did that? *Who the hell did that?*

Before the thought was complete, her fingers were flying over the keyboard. And hitting Tweet.

Aw @jaredcombs I'm sorry. I told u size didn't matter & these things happen 2 a lot of men. But I understand.

And below? A photo of his itty-bitty willy.

That'll teach you to sext a picture of your dick, you son of a bitch.

Immature? Yes. Vindictive? Yup. Felt good? Most definitely.

But in moments the golden glow of revenge started to fade, leaving behind the bright, pulsing red of hurt and humiliation.

Damn, it hurt.

She tossed the cell back in her purse and ground the heels of her palms to her eyes, surely smearing her carefully applied eye makeup.

They hadn't been in love, but she'd cared for him. Thought he'd at least held some affection for her. Why did this crap always happen to her? Growing up with her parents, she should have a built-in radar for bullshit, lies, and betrayal.

Should. If she only had a pair of boots for every "should" in her life.

Pressure pushed against her sternum like a fist, tears burning her eyes. But lowering her hands, she blinked like an Oklahoma dust storm had suddenly rolled across the sidewalk. The hell if she'd let one drop fall for that jerk.

"Oh damn," she muttered, glaring at her keys, which seemed to mock her from the sidewalk where they'd tumbled from her nerveless fingers. Groaning, she bent down and curled her fingers around the metal key ring, nails scraping the pavement.

Pop. Pop.

Gunshots.

OhGodohGodohGod.

Her purse hit the ground. Her ass quickly followed suit. Asphalt bit into her skin through her skirt, but she couldn't move. Couldn't breathe.

Growing up in the quiet town of Weston, she'd never heard that heart-stopping percussion of a bullet leaving a barrel. But she'd spent many hours in Addy's Dorchester apartment and had heard her fair share of gunshots over the years. And after nine seasons of *Criminal Minds*, she could identify the cracks of bullets…and the thump of metal meeting flesh.

Especially when it blasted not two feet away from her.

Everything slowed until the world moved through a thick wall of molasses.

The jerk of a tall, black man's body before he slumped boneless to the ground.

The grimace of agony and shock twisting the face turned toward her as if in a silent plea for help.

The dull, flat gleam of sunlight bouncing off a gun before it was tucked inside a coat.

Her heart raced to her throat. Lodged there and throbbed. *Oh Jesus*. She scooted closer to the tire, her palms scraping the ground.

Close your eyes, a voice screamed inside her head. *Close your eyes*. If she did, maybe she could disappear like in her dreams. Could convince herself none of this was happening. Could pretend her alarm would go off any minute, and this would be a terrible product of eating a family-size bag of M&Ms right before going to bed.

But no amount of denial could erase the image branded into her brain. Probably for the first time in Boston's history, the sidewalk was clear of morning pedestrian traffic.

Clear except for the body on the ground.

And the man standing in the mouth of the alley — with a gun in his hand.

Caucasian. Average height. Surprisingly young. Mid-to-late twenties. Closely cut light hair. Square jaw with a large, vicious, sickle-shaped scar carved into the skin.

Flat brown eyes. That stared directly at her. And then he turned and dashed away.

Stunned, horrified cries split the air as people poured out

of the coffee shop and other businesses, swarming and running over like cockroaches with the light suddenly thrown on. Frozen, she gaped at them, unable to process what she'd just witnessed. Unwilling to process it.

"Let me help you, sweetheart."

The gentle, but firm grip on her arm registered before the words did. One moment she'd been cowering on the ground, and the next, some Good Samaritan guided her to her feet. Shock robbed her knees of strength, and she leaned against her rescuer, grateful.

"Are you okay?" he asked, his other hand bracing her back.

"Y-yes," she stammered, though the answer was far from the truth. Tilting her head back, she glanced up at her Samaritan. "Thank y—"

A shard of ice the size of a glacier pierced her chest, numbing her limbs, encasing her lungs in a deep freeze so she couldn't breathe.

Hard jaw. Brutal scar. Dead eyes.

He'd circled back around. Discarded his sweatshirt and slapped on a black baseball cap. But she recognized him, even though no one else in the accumulating crowd of people did.

She tried to scream. But, as if caught in a nightmare, the cry was snarled in her throat, trapped.

Cruel fingers dug into the flesh of her arm.

"Shh," he soothed, a warm smile that failed to reach his eyes, curled his mouth, flashing a perfect, white smile except for a slightly crooked front tooth. On anyone else it would've been charming. Him, too, if she hadn't just seen him blow a man away. "Don't even think about screaming," he murmured, bowing his head over hers, his lips grazing her ear.

To an onlooker he would appear to be comforting her, not terrorizing her.

"You didn't see anything. You don't know anything. You missed everything because that tight little ass of yours was turned away, you understand me? Nod if you understand." His voice lowered, hardened, and the hold on her arm tightening to the point of pain. She whimpered. And nodded. "Good girl," he praised, then leaned closer and noisily sniffed her hair. He chuckled. "I almost wish you would open your mouth. I would enjoy coming for you. Would love catching you before I slit that pretty throat."

Why didn't anyone notice what was happening? She was surrounded by people, and had never been so alone, so isolated. So damn afraid.

"Remember what I said," he warned once more before his grasp eased, and then he disappeared.

With a strangled sob, she sank to the ground, her knees finally giving out. She didn't move from her crouch next to the tire. Not when the cold from the sidewalk seeped through her clothes and into her skin. Not when sirens wailed in the air. Not even when one of Boston's finest stooped down beside her and asked if she'd been hit or needed to go to the hospital.

Hospital? What could they do for her? Could they turn back the clock? Erase her memories?

No, they couldn't.

A man had been killed just feet away from her.

And she'd just been threatened by his murderer.

God*damn*, birthdays sucked.

Chapter Two

THREE MONTHS LATER

She hadn't changed.

Through his windshield, Shane Roarke studied the front of The Grease Spot—who in the hell had come up with that god-awful name for a diner?—and the petite woman who just exited the entrance.

And as he'd done in the last couple of days since he'd started tailing Fallon from her apartment to work and back to her home, he tried to focus on the fact that she appeared to have no sense of self-preservation as she strolled out of the restaurant, not even scanning the dark street to check if anyone who didn't belong lurked nearby. Tried to dredge up irritation that instead of having her keys at the ready, she paused next to that ridiculous toy she called a car and rummaged in her purse for several long moments. Tried to conjure anger that she didn't even notice him parked behind her, damn near kissing her bumper.

He tried. Oh the fury was there, simmering at her complete lack of self-awareness. But after seeing her for the first time in over a year, rage wasn't the prevalent emotion.

It was riding backseat to his dick.

Some part of him should be ashamed of lusting after a woman with the face of an angel and who'd been his little sister's best friend for over a decade.

Should.

But Fallon wasn't his sister—as much as he insisted on telling her and himself—and she damn sure was no angel.

Closing his eyes, he pinched the bridge of his nose. In that sandbox called Afghanistan, he would sometimes alleviate stress and pressure by performing deep breathing techniques his battle buddy and childhood friend, Marcus Ramirez, insisted he learn.

Slowly inhale through the nose, bringing it from the gut. Work the breath up to the head and exhale out the mouth. Repeat.

He opened his eyes.

Nope. Still hard as hell.

Giving in to the need, he greedily studied her skin like liquid gold. Her ridiculously gorgeous honey-and-chocolate curls. Dove-gray eyes. Delicate facial bones. A wide, bordering-on-lascivious mouth that might inspire heavenly sonnets, but a body men wrote Cinemax skin flicks about, not poems. And she kissed...fuck. She kissed like a sinner, not a saint. A sinner who enjoyed it. Just one crush of lips and tangle of tongues seven years ago, and he still remembered her taste. Sunshine and sex. The way she'd licked his lips, sucked hard and hungry on his tongue... Only his mother and sister in the next room had prevented him from shoving Fallon to her knees and discovering if she could curl her tongue around his cock just as prettily.

Well, his family's presence, and the fact that she was Fallon.

Impulsive, cheeky, whimsical Fallon. His little sister's best friend and a female Peter Pan, forever young, never growing up. And totally wrong for him. He'd recognized it the night of her eighteenth birthday when she'd ambushed him with a kiss in his mother's kitchen, and nothing in the time since had changed his mind.

His cock might be all on board the damn-the-consequences-and-fuck-her train, but his brain still retained enough working cells to register that becoming involved with her would only lead to catastrophe. He harbored no doubt that sex with Fallon would be something like tossing a match in a bucket of gasoline, but when it eventually burned out—and it would; it always did—what then? When lust could no longer cloak the dissimilarities that marked them as different as oil and water. There would be hurt and bad feelings—even more than existed between them now. And he would hate for Fallon and Addisyn's relationship to be affected by the fallout.

Yeah, Fallon had to remain hands off.

Clenching said hands around the steering wheel, he strong-armed his thoughts back to Fallon's protection and away from all things naked. She finally opened her door and entered the car. He waited until another vehicle pulled behind her before easing away from the curb and following. The drive from the diner to her Allston apartment was short—ten minutes. As she slid into a spot on the side of the three-story brick building, he parked across the street with a direct, unhindered view of the entrance.

Glass door with double panes on each side.

Flimsy green, wire fence that ran from the entrance and edged the sidewalk.

While Shane had finished up outstanding items on his desk earlier that day, Khalil Jordan, one of his three business partners in their security firm GDG Security Solutions, had conducted reconnaissance on Fallon's apartment building. His report had relayed that the security camera over the door was just for show, and the tenants didn't require a key or code to unlock the front door. It was a free-for-all for whoever wanted to enter the dwelling.

Why the hell was she living in such a dump? When Addisyn had called three days ago to inform him about Fallon witnessing a gangland hit, she hadn't mentioned her friend's living situation. His sister had told him about Fallon being fired from her job at an event-planning company after the murder, but she couldn't have found better employment than that eyesore of a diner? Something that paid well enough so she could afford better than this place? Surely, her father was helping her financially. Or better yet, with a sociopathic murderer on her ass, why hadn't she moved in with her father at his Beacon Hill brownstone? Nothing added up.

But then again, this was Fallon. The same logic that would prevent her from asking her very wealthy parent for help was the same that had her insistent about depending on the overworked and underpaid Boston PD for protection for the last three months instead of calling on him. Him, who handled private security for a living.

He snorted, more than a little irritated. Thank God his sister had finally wised up and ignored her best friend's insane demands for secrecy. Of course it'd taken her noticing a suspicious car sitting outside Fallon's apartment for two nights in a row for her to make that call to him.

In the two days and nights he and his team had been trailing Fallon, he hadn't noticed anyone watching her or him, but that little fact did nothing to lessen his frustration at Fallon or his sister.

Fallon exited her car, slinging her purse over her shoulder. The gesture struck him as...weary. No. He studied the slight droop of her shoulders, the customary buoyancy and energy missing from her step as she rounded the corner of the parking lot.

Not weary.

Defeated.

Something inside him leaped and snarled. In the eleven years he'd known Fallon, he'd experienced the full gamut of her emotional range. Defiant. Mischievous. Jovial. Angry. Even sorrowful. But never defeated. On her it was... blasphemous.

The first time he'd seen a man die, Shane had almost lost the burger and fries he'd eaten at the chow hall earlier that evening. The crimson stain of spilled blood. The unnatural stillness. The sick, soul-staining knowledge that he'd taken a life. A taint—a memory—that couldn't be washed away by years of service and sacrifice.

But he'd been a soldier, charged with defending his country on foreign soil. Weapons, facing attacks, and yes, death, were expected parts of his time in the military. Fallon had just been starting another workday, buying coffee... She never should've been brushed by the ugliness of this world. Never should've had to witness the cruelty men could inflict on one another. Never should have to be forever tainted with the memory of murder.

If he could, he would steal that knowledge from her, lock it away so it couldn't touch her. But while he was three months too late to do that, he could still protect her.

As Fallon neared the short walk to the entrance, he noticed two shadows separating from the darkness surrounding the neighboring apartment building. Between one moment and the next, he eased from the vehicle, the disabled interior light not betraying his presence to the pair stealing up the sidewalk. Jerking the short brim of his knit cap lower, he circled the back end, soundlessly keeping pace with them across the street.

Two males. Caucasian. Average height. Both about 160-170 pounds. Dark-colored hoodies, jeans. Light from the streetlamp they passed under bounced off a black gun. 9mm in the right hand of the male on the left. Shane lifted his hand to his shoulder holster, his thumb grazing the brake. No. It would be safer to defuse the situation rather than adding another weapon to the mix.

He blanked his mind. Shut out everything but disarming and neutralizing the two men closing in on Fallon. A calm descended, leveling his pulse, steadying his heartbeat. He stalked across the street, sticking to the black pockets outside the streetlamp's exposing glare.

In seconds he stood behind the unarmed punk. Barely pausing, Shane slammed his booted heel into the back of the asshole's knee. With a shocked and agonized scream, the male crumbled toward the ground. The back of Shane's fist to the guy's jaw accelerated the fall.

As the satisfying *thud* of skull meeting pavement echoed in the night, the armed assailant whirled around, gun outstretched in his right hand.

Shane was already moving.

He snapped out his left hand, shoving the gun aside even as he shifted to the right and out of the line of fire. Simultaneously, he rotated closer, gripped the weapon with both hands. In one sinuous motion, he forced the barrel toward the kid, wrist-locking the hand clutching the gun. The scarred, tight muscles in his back spasmed, protesting at the abrupt, fluid motion. He ground his teeth against the twinge of pain and maintained his steady hold.

"Fuck, man!" the guy wailed as his knees buckled, and he strained against Shane's hold. The cry broke off sharply when the barrel nudged his chin. His eyes widened until the whites nearly eclipsed the dark centers. "Okay, man, okay…"

"Get down on your face, motherfucker," Shane ordered, voice cold. The gun didn't waver as he stood over the man who'd intended to snatch Fallon's life so remorselessly.

Gritting his teeth, he eclipsed the rising anger before it could engulf him. He couldn't afford that right now. Not with two dangerous thugs stretched out at his feet. Because he didn't doubt their identity. Even before the cuff of the guy's sleeve rode up the arms extended above his head, revealing the L and W tattooed on his skin.

The Lords of War.

Compared to the Bloods, the Avenue King Crips, and Gangsta Disciples, the Lords of War were a relatively young gang. But in the last five years, they'd grown fast—over two thousand members strong—and were responsible for a good part of the drug and firearms trafficking in Boston. As far as brutality, mercilessness, and greed were concerned, the Lords were right up there with the Crips and Bloods.

And Fallon had witnessed their leader, Jonah Michaels, carry out a hit.

"You don't know who I run with do you, bitch? This ain't over. You don't know who you just fucked with," the Lords of War gang member snarled from the ground, having recouped his balls since the gun no longer kissed his face. "You and the bitch—"

"Shut the fuck up," Shane growled, pressing a knee into the asshole's spine. Tapping his Bluetooth earpiece, he slid the weapon into his waistband, then removed a zip tie from his coat pocket, and quickly secured the still-cursing male's wrists at the small of his back. When Shane finished repeating the action with his ankles, Ciaran Ross's deep greeting resounded in his ear.

"I need a cleanup. The front of Fallon's building." Shane moved to the unconscious male on the ground and flipped him over. "Come in black," Shane ordered the ex-DEA agent-turned-security-specialist, using their code to approach in stealth mode.

"Copy that. ETA three minutes," Ciaran confirmed.

With another press to his earpiece, Shane ended the call and made short work of binding the other man's arms and legs.

Only then did he allow himself to glance toward the apartment complex's entrance. Only then did he permit the ice encasing his emotions to thaw. Only then did he admit that for the first time since a bullet had ripped through his flesh, leaving him staring up at a dark, star-scattered night as his blood pumped onto a foreign street, he was afraid.

If Addisyn hadn't called him. If he hadn't followed Fallon home. If he'd been seconds slower…

A shiver rippled through him.

Fallon emerged from her crouch in the corner of the small porch, making herself as small a target as possible during the fight. She lifted her gaze from the sidewalk where her two would-be assassins lay. Shock darkened her gray eyes until they appeared black. A soft, weak sound escaped her as she wrapped her arms around herself.

Her lips trembled.

Parted.

"Umm…hi?"

Chapter Three

Fallon blinked.

Blinked again.

Nope. Shane Roarke still stood at her living room window.

His tall frame and wide shoulders nearly swamped the pane and glass. Hard muscle strained at the black cotton of his long-sleeved shirt. And as he edged the curtain aside to peer outside, a delicious display of strength shifted beneath his shirt. She focused on that subtle show of lethal grace, latched onto it with a desperation that had panic attack scrawled all over it. In bright red Crayola crayons.

Oh Jesus. She squeezed her eyes shut, but immediately that big, ugly gun in Shane's hands flashed across the backs of her lids. *No!* Her eyes popped open. *Bad move, bad move.*

She returned her gaze to Shane's back. As long as she fixated on the prime example of badassery in front of her, she could shove aside the fact that she'd been seconds away from becoming a tear on some gangbanger's cheek. Did they still do that? She clasped her hands together on her lap, the grip so tight her fingers throbbed in protest. Wow, she had to cut back on the *Lockup* marathons.

"I take it the guys who arrived after your phone call were friends of yours?" Three figures dressed in all black and wearing ski masks had seemingly materialized out of the darkness bare minutes after Shane had put the two men on the ground. Like silent wraiths, the eerie trio had soundlessly hauled the assailants to their feet, threw them over their shoulders, and disappeared as quietly as they'd appeared. If she hadn't peeped it with her own eyes, she wouldn't have believed they'd been there at all.

"Yes," Shane replied without turning away from the window.

"What will they do with those two?" She swallowed, trepidation suddenly necklacing her throat. Which was crazy since they obviously hadn't cared about her well-being. "Will they kill them?"

This gained his attention. He slowly pivoted, his eyes zeroing in on her. She should've braced herself for the impact of it. Even with the stress of the last hour stretching her tighter than a taut guitar string, she should've been more prepared for the powerful impact of that intent stare.

He and Addy shared the same astonishing turquoise eyes that belonged only in those over-the-top contact-lens ads or in teen vampire movies. But while her friend's gentle, blue-green shade reminded Fallon of sparkling Caribbean seas, Shane's sharper, incisive stare called to mind the gem with the same color. Even the thick, ridiculously long lashes couldn't soften the hardness in that gaze. But then everything about him was hard.

Close-cut black hair emphasized the angular planes that kept his face from verging into way-too-pretty-for-a-man land. The stern line of his full, sinfully curved mouth. The strong chest and solid thighs that whispered of power and unshakable control. The black long-sleeved shirt, cargo pants, and boots in no way concealed the animal magnetism of a body that was sculpted for a Spartan cape and loincloth. They enhanced it.

"No, they won't kill them. The two men *who tried to execute you tonight* will be interrogated and then turned over to the police."

"Shouldn't we have called the cops first? Isn't it their job to 'interrogate'?" She stressed the term, bristling at his tone and reminder of her near miss of starring on an episode of *48 Hours: Hard Evidence*.

Shane snorted. "You have such faith in the police—such faith you didn't immediately call me when all this went down. When it was the same cops who obviously leaked your name to the Lords of War and didn't even have the courtesy to call and give you a heads-up that your identity had been compromised." He crossed his arms. "As for your question, no, I'm not calling them first. Their hands are tied by rules that don't apply to me."

A gleam entered his eyes, and a pit big enough for her heart to plummet through yawned wide in her stomach. She wasn't an idiot. The thought that tonight had been somehow connected to the murder she'd witnessed had occurred to her. Yet, denial and fear had her shaking her head. "You don't know for certain tonight had anything to do with Jonah Michaels. It could've been a mugging, and I was in the wrong place at the wrong time."

A dark eyebrow winged high. "In a semi-lighted place where anyone could either be leaving the apartment or arriving? They didn't even try to accost or rip you off. Their purpose was to take you out. It wasn't a mugging, Fallon. It was a failed assassination attempt. And only two reasons why come to mind. You are the only eyewitness to a hit. And they want to make damn sure you're not alive to testify."

She shot to her feet, crossing her arms and rubbing her skin through her white shirt. Three months ago, she'd never heard of Jonah Michaels or the Lords of War. She'd had no clue that a daily stop in a coffee shop would end up in her witnessing a turf-war execution. Terrified but resolved to perform her civic duty even in spite of Michaels's threat the day of the shooting, she'd picked the hit man, Jonah Michaels, out of a lineup and agreed to testify with the promise from the Boston PD and district attorney that her name and personal information would be kept under wraps.

"I don't get it. Three months have passed and no sign of trouble. Why wouldn't the cops contact me?"

"It's possible it took Jonah Michaels and his crew that long to find out your name. Or it's possible the detective on your case and the DA don't know your identity has been compromised. But damn it, Fallon, the police force is known for leaking like a sieve." His eyes narrowed. "Which brings me to my next question. Why did I have to hear about your witnessing a murder that happened *three months ago* from my sister instead of you? Why didn't you come to me? *Three months ago*."

Really? She fought not to laugh in his face. Oh, it could be the fact that if Shane could help it, he didn't remain in the same room with her for any length of time. Ever since The Kiss, he'd avoided her like Montezuma's revenge.

The kiss.

Their relationship could be separated into two eras: BK and AK. Before Kiss and After Kiss. High on turning eighteen and officially emerging out of the jailbait category, she'd cornered Shane in his family's kitchen, fisted his shirt, plastered her breasts to his chest, and crushed her mouth to his. With him home on leave, she'd refused to pass up the opportunity to find out how her girlhood crush kissed. For one blissful moment, his firm mouth had softened, parted. His tongue had breached her lips, sweeping inside, and taking control of a kiss that segued from fumbling sweetness to blistering hot in under a nanosecond. God, even now she could feel those blunt fingertips digging into her hips, dragging her close as he ground the steely, freaking huge length of his cock against the pad of her pussy, directly over her clit. Like then, she shuddered. He'd been hot and hard for her. *Her*. Delighted and breathless, she'd pressed closer, moaned, then—nothing.

One moment she'd been drowning in her first real taste of sensual pleasure, and the next she'd been left standing alone, stunned, aching, and trembling with his terse "Not interested" ringing in her ears. He'd crushed her that night. If not in words, then definitely with actions. Her parents had told her they weren't interested her entire life. With Addy, Shane, and their mother, Trudy, she'd believed she'd finally found people who were. Especially Shane, who'd become her knight in shining armor, her fairy-tale prince whom she'd been in love with for years. His rejection in such blunt terms—it'd cauterized a hope and dream that had been fragile but so sweet. From that night forward, her head and heart had registered Shane's dismissal. But her body had yet to get on the same he's-just-not-that-into-you program.

Really, in hindsight, she should be thankful he torpedoed her fantasies of "forever." But just like Shane didn't "do" her, she didn't "do" forevers.

Long ago, Addy had confided in her about the wear and tear her and Shane's childhood had taken on him. He'd become an adult way too early, compensating for a mother cursed with Peter Pan syndrome. As a result, he desired what he'd been deprived of as a boy. A home—a real home. With a wife and children.

Exactly what she could never give him.

Or more accurately, what she didn't want to give him—or anyone. Marriage was for other people whose earliest memories weren't of their parents arguing over their mother's boyfriends—plural. Marriage was for the people whose mothers didn't switch husbands as often as the changing of the guard at Buckingham Palace. For people who didn't mind risking their heart and emotional heath on someone and then face total devastation when the other person left. Because if she'd learned one thing from her parents' marriage and her mother's merry-go-round relationships, it was that someone always left.

Nope, Shane had sliced and diced her heart with a rusty knife, but he'd reminded her of a core knowledge she'd temporarily forgotten under the haze of puppy love.

Still…prior to her impulsively jumping him, he'd been her friend. He'd teased her, cared for her, watched over her. Afterward, he'd transformed into a polite, distant stranger. But not only had he changed—she'd been irrevocably altered, too. Shane had granted her an all-too-brief glimpse of true hunger. Not in the seven years following had she tasted such sensual delight again. No man since had been able to conjure the molten swirl of pleasure in her belly or that specific rhythm in her pulse. No man had pushed her to the verge of orgasm with just one kiss. No man had elicited the need to climb up his body like a spider monkey in heat and cling, claw, and scream.

Only him.

In the most real way, Shane had ruined her for other men. With. One. Freaking. Kiss.

The bastard. She scowled.

"You know why," she said, resenting him for making her admit even that much. "What were you doing here tonight anyway? Somehow I don't think it was a coincidence."

He slid his hands into the front pockets of his cargo pants, and the dark cotton strained over his powerful thighs. Not that she was looking…not really.

"I was here for you," he simply stated.

Over a year. Thirteen months to be exact. The length of time between now and the last time she'd seen Shane at Addy's master's graduation ceremony. Still, no matter how much time had passed, those five words sent an illicit tingle through her veins, hardening her nipples and pooling in the flesh between her legs. Her brain comprehended the platonic meaning of his statement, but her body—her stubborn, slow-on-the-uptake body—interpreted something hotter, steamier. Naughtier.

She shot a glare down at her traitorous breasts, her scowl deepening. *He's not here for* you, *damn it*.

So since he'd proven he couldn't stand being in her

company, his presence begged two questions:

A. Why was he still standing in her apartment?

And B. What the hell did "I was here for you" mean?

She scoffed, throwing him a disbelieving glance as she fell back on old habits. When in doubt, antagonize.

"If you were truly 'here for me,' you would have a Kahlua in one hand and Henry Cavill's number in the other. Since I'm not having drunken phone sex with Superman, there must be another reason you're darkening my living room."

Of course, he displayed no reaction. She heaved a loud, exaggerated sigh that could've parted Donald Trump's toupee right down the middle. That's right. Mr. I Am the Law didn't do humor.

Didn't do her either, for that matter.

"Addisyn called me a few days ago."

"Ohhh," she drawled, throwing her hands up in the air. "And there it is. I should've known."

"She feels like something hasn't been right lately. She didn't want to worry you, but she hasn't been able to shake the feeling of being watched. And last night, while she was over here, she glanced out the living room window, and thought she saw someone sitting in a car across the street. And when she left, the car was still there, the person inside."

A shudder worked its way down Fallon's spine at the thought of an unknown "someone" lurking outside her building.

"*She* shouldn't have had to call me," Shane continued. He removed his hands and stalked across the room, eliminating the distance between them in several long strides. In seconds he loomed over her, his clean, fresh scent that reminded her of crisp, autumn nights enveloping her even as a fierce frown creased his brow. "You should have contacted me when this all first went down. Of course I heard about Jonah Michaels being indicted for murder on the news, but I never imagined you were involved in this somehow. Damn it, Fallon. Protection is what I do for a living. I should've been the first person you called."

"Of course," she agreed, the sweetness in her tone as phony as Kim Kardashian's shiny new ass. "Because we're so close. Because we're BFFs. Because on the rare times we do manage to occupy the same space, you treat me like I'm an escapee from a leprosy colony. How could I have not called you?"

"That's ridiculous," he snapped. "And I don't care if you were a carrier for the goddamn plague. You. Should've. Called. Me. Your life was at stake. To hell with feelings."

And didn't that just sting?

Forcing a smile, she shifted back a step. "How right you are. As usual, I got caught up in my feelings instead of using my common sense. How silly and *female* of me." An ominous rumble rolled in his chest, but she smiled broadly and wondered if it looked as bogus as it felt. "Well," she clapped her hands in mock delight, "thanks for the save tonight, but I'm pretty worn out from all the…excitement. If you don't mind?" She nodded her head in the direction of the front door, desperate to get him out of her home. Desperate to get rid of him before she did something incredibly stupid like ask him, *Why don't you want me? Why am I not good enough for you? Can you touch me?* She shuddered. Yeah, he had to go. "It's getting late." Actually, it couldn't be later than nine o'clock, but… "Night."

He didn't move. Except to cross his arms. "I'm not going

anywhere. Consider me your personal security detail for the night."

Shock coldcocked her. "Wh-what?" she stuttered. "Y-you can't stay here. With me."

Again, the arch of a dark brow. "You're welcome to try and put me out."

For a quick second, the thought of putting her hands on that hard chest, of having those firm, sexy muscles flex under her palms, of having those strong arms wrapped around her, pressing her against... *Oh for the love of—* "Shane, this isn't necessary. Unless..." Her voice trailed off as a terrifying idea leaped into her head, stealing her breath. "Do you think"—she swallowed, propelled the words past her suddenly constricted throat—"are you expecting someone else to show up? To finish...?"

"No." He strode forward and encircled her upper arms in an implacable grip. "Look at me." Pinching her chin, he tilted her head up so she didn't have a choice but to obey him. His jeweled gaze bore into hers. "I don't believe anyone will come after you again tonight. They wouldn't risk attempting two hits in one night. It would draw too much attention. Even if they did," he said, his touch tightening. "I have a man outside your building, and I'm here. You're safe. No one will get to you. I promise you that."

Relief coursed through her in a heady flood. And it was the deluge of emotion that convinced her to give in.

One night—what was the harm in one night?

Wrapping her fingers around his wrists, she sank into him. Assured by his strength, by the fire lighting his bright gaze. "Okay." She nodded. "Okay."

But even as she agreed and headed to the linen closet for

sheets and blankets to make up the couch for her overnight guest, she glanced up at the textured, water-stained ceiling.

Why did she suddenly feel like Chicken Little waiting for a piece of the sky to plummet and knock her the hell out?

Chapter Four

Fallon flopped onto her back, tossing the suffocating weight of the sheet aside. Any other night, she would've cracked the window to allow the cool, refreshing late-spring breeze in the room. But that was before she'd almost become a statistic. Now the window remained firmly shut, and though the warmth in the bedroom neared stifling, she refused to open it. Common sense railed that unless a possible assailant had been bitten and injected with arachnid DNA, no way could someone scale the brick building to break into her third-floor window.

Still…

With a huff of breath, she rolled over, stared at the far wall and the scintillating view of her clothes thrown over a chair. One a.m. The digital clock seemed to taunt her as the quiet crowded in on her. It pressed down until the silence reverberated in her chest, her ears, covered her like the sheet she'd just thrown aside. Heavy, smothering. And it didn't help that every sense seemed to hover on high alert. As if even the very nerves in her body acknowledged that just a room away, Shane Roarke slept on her couch. Possibly naked. All that golden skin on display, begging to be licked, tasted, savored…

A hot pulse settled low in her stomach and spread its sensual, sneaky fingers to all points north and south. Especially south. Her nipples beaded beneath the thin cotton of her T-shirt, and she clenched her hands to prevent her fingers from inching underneath the top to soothe—or aggravate—the ache. But nothing could prevent her from squeezing her thighs together. From ratcheting the ache in her sex from a pulse to a steady throb.

She closed her eyes, flung an arm above her head, and trailed her fingertips over the path of skin left bare by the high-riding hem of her shirt and the band of her sleep shorts. Shivering, she substituted her touch for the phantom man looming over her in the darkness. No, not a phantom man. Shane. Behind her eyelids, his gaze blazed down on her. His rough, deep breathing echoed in her ears, telegraphing the lust that hardened his beautiful, warrior's face into a sexual mask. Calloused fingers trailed the edge of her shorts, dipped beneath, sought damp flesh…

"Oh damn," Fallon muttered, leaping from the bed as if flames had erupted from beneath the mattress. Masturbating while the object of her dirty fantasies lay only feet away? And with his damn bionic hearing, he would probably catch every sigh or moan. *Jesus Christ.* She scrubbed her palms down her face. This wasn't going to work. Sleep was a nonfactor.

Tension. Belated adrenaline rush. Freaking nerves. All

of the above could be attributed to her edginess. Not Shane's sudden appearance. She'd gotten over her silly childhood crush seven years ago on her eighteenth birthday, after she'd been slapped down by the cold rejection from the man she'd idealized and loved.

Love. Hah. What a crock. More like candy-coated teenage lust. Love was fodder for movie tickets and romance novels. She didn't dream of the house with the white picket fence, two-point-five-kids, and a minivan in the driveway. Inevitably, the house would be a pickup site for weekend custody exchanges, the kids would become casualties in a divorce battle, and the van would be traded in for a screaming-red, midlife crisis convertible.

Besides, she didn't go for stern, inflexible, my-way-or-the-highway men. Okay, sure Jared had been a flake, but at least he knew how to relax, have fun. Freaking laugh.

So Shane had no reason to avoid her like the plague. She had no intention of repeating history by throwing herself at him.

And she'd prove it.

She left her bedroom and made a pit stop at the linen closet to grab a sheet before continuing toward the living room. She'd forgotten to give him one before heading to her bedroom for the night…okay, *escaping* to her room. Still, the belated offering seemed as good of an excuse as any to seek him out.

Light from the television cast flickering shadows across the floor, coffee table, and sofa. And the man stretched out on the cushions.

Oh Jesus, Mary, Joseph…

The piece of furniture appeared Lilliputian under his

long frame. One large, well-formed foot balanced on the couch arm, while the other rested on the floor. Even relaxed in sleep, muscles corded his thighs, his power and ability delineated in every tendon. Her breath stalled and stuttered in her lungs, lust climbing her insides like a twisting, clinging vine. It didn't require much imagination to envision those firm legs pressing hers wider, controlling her movements with an ease and strength that set her heart to pounding... and her panties to melting.

She enjoyed pretty things—cars, clothes, shoes, jewelry. Of course, since striking out on her own, she couldn't fit most of those into her tiny budget, but it didn't suppress her love of them. Beautifying the ordinary, bringing the fantasy to vivid life all played into her dream of owning an event-planning company one day.

The male dwarfing her sofa didn't need embellishment. With a chain and dog tags resting on his collarbone and tight black boxer briefs hugging his upper thighs, he exuded a sexual magnetism that reached out to her like a primal mating call. Hell, she was two seconds away from rubbing her thighs together like a freakin' cricket.

Disgust at her wayward libido pricked at her pride, but it didn't stop her lascivious perusal. The man might possess the verbosity and rigidity of a Spartan warrior, but *Jesus Christ*, he had the body of one, too. It was a living work of art. Hard contours, defined ridges, enticing planes and dips. He could've been chiseled by a master's loving and meticulous hand. Even the propped up foot was well formed, and utterly masculine. Speaking of masculine...

A rush of heat blazed a path from her belly, up her chest, and poured into her face. God knew, it wasn't polite to stare at a man's—especially a sleeping man's—package, but Godzilla could've been spotted off the eastern shore, and she wouldn't have been able to tear her enthralled scrutiny away.

The black cotton couldn't conceal the large, impressive bulge that lined his thigh. With his legs parted, she had an excellent view of just how far down that bulge reached. Which was long enough to have her sex clenching in excitement and trepidation. Good God, he wasn't even *aroused*. She pressed a trembling hand to her stomach. What would he look like fully erect, hard, tip flushed and glistening, ready to…?

Beneath the briefs, his cock stirred. Flexed. Lengthened.

Gasping, she jerked her gaze to his face. And collided with a searing, bright stare. A hungry stare.

She blinked. Surely the lust she believed she'd glimpsed had been her sex-deprived imagination. Because Shane didn't think of her as a woman—a desirable woman. He didn't want her, his little sister's best friend. He'd made that abundantly clear.

And yet…yet, he continued to lie there, studying her from beneath thick, ridiculously long lashes, his eyes a rim of hot turquoise. Tension invaded his limbs. And his dick…

Swallowing, she once again wrenched her attention back to his face.

"I, uh," she stammered, glanced down, and thrust her arm toward him. "Sheet?"

Instead of replying, he swung his foot off the couch to join the other on the floor and sat. And that quick, the reserved, distant, familiar Shane returned. His sharp, incisive scrutiny scanned from her wild bed-head, down her bare legs to her feet. As his inventory reversed direction, her toes curled into the threadbare carpet. The visual survey had been cold, impersonal. Yet, the quiver in her sex felt very *personal*.

"Can't sleep?" he asked.

"No," she murmured, her arm falling to her side. "It's too quiet."

He nodded, rising to his feet. The dog tags around his neck clacked against one another, drawing her attention to the wide, naked expanse of his chest. How she managed to sound calm and unaffected by the sight of all that taut skin should be filed under minor miracles. Especially since inside her panties she popped, sizzled, and lit up like a damn Fourth of July fireworks show.

"Here." He scooped up the television remote from the coffee table and tossed it to her. "Take the couch." He bent, picked up his pants, and turned to step into them. "I'll sleep on the—"

"*Jesus Christ*." She caught the remote on autopilot, the sheet dropping from her numb fingers. Horror poured through her in a thick, choking deluge. Before her mind could catch up with her body, she was closing the distance between them. Her hands were reaching for him, gripping his hips above the low-hanging black band of his boxers and unbuckled, sagging pants.

Her eyes were drinking in the terrible scars marring his back.

Shane went unnaturally still, and the tensing of his muscles telegraphed his intention to jerk away. But she tightened her hold, ignored the fact that she'd violated his unspoken edict regarding her touching him.

"Please," she whispered, unable to prevent the pain and fear from seeping through. Maybe he detected it, detected the desperate need. Because, though he didn't relax, instead remaining as rigid as a statue, he didn't move away from her. Didn't leave her.

Emitting a sound caught somewhere between a whimper and a sigh, she gently—reverently—traced the gouged-out flesh just below his waist, the hard, puckered skin surrounding the old wound. Pressing her forehead to his shoulder blade, she smoothed fingertips over the long, ridged scar aligning the bottom of his spine. Stroked the raised, shiny mark the size and shape of a nickel on the back of his upper arm.

Grief for his suffering, panic at the realization of just how close she'd come to losing him pummeled the breath from her chest, leaving a hollow, agonizing ache behind. Of course she'd known he'd been hurt; only a serious injury could've kept Shane from returning to the Army he loved. But four years ago when she'd received that call from Addy about Shane being shipped home, her friend had told her he'd been shot. That's it. She hadn't detailed the gravity the scars covering his body conveyed. They'd kept her in the dark. Purposefully.

"You wouldn't let me come to the hospital," she said.

"No," he stated, voice flat.

"Why?" she demanded softly. He didn't reply, only fisted his fingers at his sides. "I would've come. If you'd let me, I would've," she murmured, then bent and brushed her lips over the scar on his waist.

Jolting as if struck by a bolt of lightning, he whipped around, a fierce frown darkening his face. "What the hell are you doing?" he growled.

Slowly, she straightened, the truth glued to her tongue.

She hadn't paused to debate the gesture but had acted on impulse. And need. A need born of the many times in her childhood when her hurts and scars had never been kissed or even acknowledged. Her mother had been too preoccupied with the next husband, aka victim, and her father had been busy at work. Even as a little girl, she'd realized the simple act of lips to a bruise or scrape wouldn't magically erase the sting or ache. It was the attention that soothed the sting. The love and caring that said, *I can't make the pain go away, but I would take your hurt into me if I could.*

Shane wouldn't have allowed his mother to tend to his wounds. When Fallon had first met him, he'd been a mature, contained eighteen-year-old. And even back then she'd had the feeling he'd been that way for a long time. After meeting Trudy Roarke, she understood why. Though affectionate and loving, Shane and Addy's mother hadn't been the most... reliable or stable. Shane had been the adult in that family.

Lying in a hospital bed, enduring unimaginable pain, he'd probably still been the one to comfort his mother and sister, not permitting them to baby him.

He deserved to have someone fuss over him. Deserved to have someone kiss his scrapes.

But explaining that to him—telling him she'd only wanted to take away his pain—wouldn't go over well. Not at all.

Instead, she shrugged a shoulder. "I didn't—"

"Think," he snapped. "You don't think before you act." He snatched up his shirt and, yanking it over his head, strode from the living room.

"Well, ouch, damn it."

In spite of her flippant response, his harsh words sliced into her, and she swiftly worked to cauterize the wounds before they bled freely. Only Shane could inflict that kind of damage. Not her parents; she loved them, but after years and years of carelessness and emotional negligence, Fallon had built an immunity to their thoughtless cuts to her heart and spirit.

Shane, though, he still retained that power.

"Look," she continued when he reentered the room several moments later, carrying a cup, "I know spending the night in my apartment on my couch isn't how you envisioned passing your time—"

"You don't know anything," he interrupted. That aggravating icy calm had returned to his voice—and belied the hard shove of the warm mug into her hand. The aromatic scent of peppermint floating to her nose halted the acerbic comment hovering on her tongue. Tea. He'd made her tea.

"Thank you," she murmured then sipped. Humming, she closed her eyes, savoring the minty flavor and the comforting, warm slide of liquid down her throat. She opened her eyes and found Shane seated in the chair next to the sofa, his shadowed, unwavering gaze focused on where her mouth rested on the rim of the cup. For a long, taut instant, she didn't move, didn't breathe. The heaviness of his stare could've been tactile, brushing over her lips, caressing them...

Finally, when her lungs started to rebel at the lack of oxygen, his intent study lifted to her eyes. She could read nothing in the shuttered, turquoise depths. Releasing a trembling sigh, she lowered the mug.

"I don't regret being here, Fallon," he said in his low, controlled tone. "Like I said before, I wish you would've called me, not Addisyn."

"So you said." She peered down into the steaming dark brown liquid. "But I didn't want to impose. I'm not family, and the police assured me I would be safe."

"You are—"

"Don't call me your sister again. We both know I'm not."

"—like family," he finished as if she hadn't cut him off. "And it damn sure wouldn't have been an imposition. Cases like yours are what we created GDG Security for."

GDG Security Solutions. The independent firm Shane and his friends, Ciaran Ross, Khalil Jordan, and Maddox Wright, owned and ran together. She'd always been curious about the business—a company made up of ex-military and law enforcement—and had even once purposefully driven by the brownstone on Arlington Street where the office was located. Everything she'd discovered about the firm, she'd Googled, too embarrassed to ask Addisyn and reveal her hunger about any details regarding Shane to her best friend.

"GDG." She leaned forward. "I've always wondered what it stood for."

A beat of silence. "Gold Dust Green."

Huh. "Does it mean something special?"

"In the military, it means everything's okay, good to go." Another beat of silence. "Focus, Fallon."

Irritation flashed, and she took another sip of tea. "I am focusing. Sue me for being curious. But fine. I should've called you when I decided to do something as foolish as witness a gangland hit. My bad. Next time it happens, you'll be first on my to-do list. Right under 'don't die,'" she drawled.

He didn't roll his eyes, but she suspected it was a close call.

"Agreeing to be a state's witness against a notorious

gang leader when other people probably would—and did—claim spontaneous blindness and deafness is commendable," he said. "But I'm not going to lie, Fallon, if I had a vote, I would've preferred you'd been one of those witnesses struck dumb and mute rather than have you involved with Jonah Michaels and the Lords of War. Yeah, it's brave, but damn, it seems like trouble finds you like a heat-seeking missile."

"Aaand this is my fault, how?" she asked from between gritted teeth. "Hold on, hold on," she countered, holding up a hand, palm out. "Let me guess. I'm reckless, rash, and I don't think through consequences."

How many times had she heard *those* words from him through the years?

He studied her, drumming his fingers on the arm of the chair. "Have you forgotten about buying property on the moon in case an apocalypse swept across the Earth—"

She snorted. "I was seventeen and had just finished reading *The Stand*."

"And the time you donated your first year's college tuition check to the Hurricane Katrina relief fund without your father's knowledge—"

"Really?" she demanded. "Forget it being an incredibly altruistic gesture, but I did that years ago."

Shane arched an eyebrow. "And breaking into Addy's ex-boyfriend's car and planting spoiled eggs and garbage under the seats? That was just two years ago."

Stiffening, she set her tea on the coffee table. "He was a douche who cheated on Addy and broke her heart. Was it childish? Sure. But if you're waiting for me to apologize, for-get it. Sometimes you have to go 'yippee-ki-yay' on a person who deserves it."

He stared at her. Blinked. Then slowly nodded. "Yippee-ki-yay. Got it. Next time you're in lockup and I'm trying to get you out, I'll make sure to explain your philosophy to the arresting officer. I'm sure he'll understand."

"I think I liked you better when you didn't talk so much," she grumbled, snatching up the remote control and turning on the television.

He had a point—and she hated it. But other than the anomaly with Doug the Douche, Addisyn's cheating rat-bastard ex, she'd prided herself on using her head more often now, not rushing headlong into situations with the purpose of seeking attention.

Once upon a time she'd been thirsty for someone—anyone—to notice her, to love her. But one morning in her sophomore year of college after waking up in the bed of boyfriend #4 in as many months, she'd stumbled into his bathroom, stared into the mirror above the sink, and found her mother gazing back at her—seeking affirmation and love in the false words and affections of anyone with a half-way decent line and dick.

That day, she'd walked out and vowed that if no one could love her, she would have to depend on herself to do it. No more careless relationships or reckless acts to threaten her academic and professional future. She didn't need a man or his pretty lies to validate herself. She'd buckled down, decided what she'd wanted to do with her life, and pursued it with a passion and diligence that had surprised her father and delighted Addy. And herself.

But Shane wouldn't know about any of that. He'd been deployed overseas, and then when he'd returned home, spending time with her hadn't exactly been on his to-do list.

She probably fit somewhere between waxing his short 'n' curlies and a colonoscopy.

Yet…his opinion still mattered.

And it still hurt that he couldn't see there was more to her than the rash eighteen-year-old who'd ambushed him in his mother's kitchen. How did she fight that?

A better question.

Why did she care?

. . .

The air, thick and sticky, trapped Fallon in its smothering embrace as she turned around, the movement torturously slow. The barrel of the gun seemed to expand, to fill her entire vision. She tried to shift backward, to the side, attempted to do anything to avoid that ugly, black void of death. But it followed her like the head of a striking snake. Running was useless—impossible. Her feet were fused to the ground, refusing to move.

The gun barrel started to glow an ominous red, orange, and yellow like a fire simmering in the belly of a great dragon. She opened her mouth wide, but the same air that stifled her motions seemed to fill her throat, lodging the scream in her windpipe.

Frozen, she stared as fire exploded from the end of the weapon, and the bullet sliced toward her…

"*No.*" Fallon jackknifed off the couch, the sheet she didn't remember covering herself with, tumbling to her waist. Wild, she scanned the room, frantically searching for the gun and the men who wanted to take her life. Heart striking her chest like a hammer against metal, she clutched the white cotton covering her legs. Sweat dampened her skin. Terror stole the moisture from her mouth. She shuddered, a whimper escaping her.

"Shh." A large, hard, warm palm cupped her cheek. "It's just a dream, baby. You're safe."

She latched onto Shane's hand as if it were a lifeline, an assurance in the dark that she was indeed, safe. "Hey. Look at me." The gentle but firm command reached past the jagged edges of panic and snagged onto the reason not enshrouded by the remaining vestiges of her nightmare. She met his bright, steady gaze, clung to the comfort and security in it. "It was just a dream. You're okay, baby. Breathe for me. With me. That's it." He lifted his other hand, cradled her face between his palms. Instinctively, she followed his deep, even inhalations, and eventually her breathing leveled. Her heartbeat no longer thundered in her ears like relentless waves crashing against a rocky shore.

The pad of his thumb swept the skin under her eye. "Better?"

No. "Yes."

"Good," he murmured and rose from his crouch next to her.

Alarm blared inside her, loud, harsh, violent. "No," she rasped, her grip on his wrists tightening. "Don't leave me. Please."

Yes, she was begging him to stay with her, to continue touching her. Yet, she couldn't dredge up disgust for how weak she sounded. Not when the claws of the nightmare lurked just on the fringes of her subconscious, waiting for her to become vulnerable again. Waiting to sink its talons into her once more.

He hesitated, but after a moment, lowered to the cushion beside her. The solid heat from his hip pressed into hers, but it wasn't enough. Like a little girl afraid of the monsters under her bed, she scrambled onto his lap, wrapping her arms around his neck and burying her face in the crook between his throat and shoulder. She inhaled his fresh scent, took it into herself like a lucky talisman.

"Fallon," he murmured, tone as strained and tense as the big body beneath her.

"Just for a little while," she pleaded. "Please."

A caress so light that for a moment she almost believed her desperate mind had imagined it swept down her hair. The air stilled in her lungs. Because if she had conjured it, maybe the soft stroke would come again. And it did. A strong arm curled around her back, long fingers settling on her hip. Slowly, she exhaled. Relaxed. Burrowed into the welcoming, safe haven of his chest.

Sighed.

Her lashes lowered, drowsiness creeping in to tug at her. She drifted, floating on a delicious, warm current. Quiet descended over the room, the only sounds their hushed breaths.

As she drifted back to sleep, firm lips brushed over her curls, across her forehead.

"I have you," a low voice rumbled. Vowed.

Or maybe she dreamed that, too.

Chapter Five

The weak late-morning sun struggled to beam down on Shane as he leaned against the hood of his truck outside the District A-1 station of the Boston Police Department. The breeze was surprisingly brisk for May, and several people hustled past him, hands shoved in pockets or collars jacked up around their ears as they hurried toward the front entrance of the station. A couple of officers shot him curious glances as they passed by him in the parking lot.

Run me in. He met their gazes head-on. *You'll be doing me a favor after last night.* Yeah, a little disturbing the peace charge would be the perfect excuse to avoid a repeat of the hell he'd endured the night before. Allowing the police to do his dirty work smacked of cowardice. But when a man faced down temptation that made Eve's apple look like a Little Debbie snack, he could be forgiven for contemplating running scared.

"Fuck me," he growled, crossing his arms. He deserved

a goddamn medal for the restraint he'd exhibited. Especially when Fallon had kissed the scars on his back. Scars he could've gone the rest of his existence without her ever glimpsing. A hot flash of humiliation speared him. He wasn't ashamed of his wounds. How could he be? Not when Marcus had given his life so Shane could stand here today, damaged but alive. On reflex, Shane grazed his fingers over the three dog tags concealed beneath his shirt. Two of them belonged to him, and one to Marcus. The other half of his dead friend's ID hung around his GDG partner Khalil's neck.

Still…

He hadn't wanted Fallon to ever see the marks. They represented a dark period when he'd been terrified, grieving, vulnerable. When the body he'd always considered strong and capable had been dependent on the tubes invading his flesh, and his mind and reason had been muddied by drugs. A period when he hadn't been able to see a future past the frosted glass doors of Walter Reed Army Medical Center's ICU.

If he'd had his wish, his mother and sister wouldn't have been allowed in to see him, but his CO and doctors had overruled that while he'd been under. His family's presence at his hospital bed had been out of his control, but Fallon's had not. He'd refused. Having her witness him hooked up to countless machines, helpless as a baby…weak…

Yeah, never would've been too soon for her to observe those scars. And last night…

His gut clenched at the phantom sensation of her lips caressing flesh that had been deadened to sensation since an enemy bullet had gouged out a chunk of skin and tissue. But, it'd seemed like the moment she'd pressed her mouth to him, nerve endings had regenerated and fired to life. The pleasure—the pleasure had bolted through him like he'd stuck his finger into an electrical outlet. For a moment, he'd forgotten every reason why touching her was a bad idea: little sister's best friend; different as night and day; asking for trouble if Addy ever found out.

It'd taken every scrap of control he tenuously possessed not to tangle his hand into those gorgeous curls, drag her around, crush his mouth to hers, and taste the sweet flavor he'd spent seven years trying to forget. Required every ounce of restraint not to lay her out on the couch, floor, table—hell, any flat surface would do—and sink his cock into her inch by inch.

But he hadn't. He'd walked away. Damn near ran away, needing space and a breather before he could return with a semblance of calm.

And he deserved to be fucking canonized for the sacrifice.

A memory flashed across his brain. Fallon, standing at the end of the sofa in a T-shirt that did nothing to hide the perfect thrust of her breasts and shorts that barely covered her hips and ass. Fallon, a hunger she probably wasn't even aware she revealed darkening her gray eyes. Fallon, staring at his cock like it was the Eighth Wonder of the World.

He clenched his jaw against the onslaught of lust razing a path straight to his dick.

Damn canonized. He deserved a halo and wings.

The front entrance to the police department swung open once again, and this time the man he'd come to see emerged.

Tristan Scott, Boston Police detective and Shane's childhood friend, crossed the parking lot, his long, confident stride eating up the distance. He had every right to that self-assurance. At thirty, Tristan was one of the youngest detectives on the force. He'd always known what he'd wanted for his future—to be a police officer just like his father and his grandfather. He rose steadily in the ranks of a career he loved and owned a home in South End with his beautiful fiancée of two years, Joy Sanders. Tristan had the dream—at least the dream Shane desired.

Stability. Family.

Growing up with Trudy Roarke as a mother, he appreciated the need for stability, security, and routine. While he'd never doubted his mother's love, and she'd never shorted him and Addy on affection, hugs hadn't paid the power bills or the rent. Kisses hadn't filled the refrigerator with food. And neither could erase the dread of climbing the stairs of their South End apartment building, afraid to look at the door in case another eviction notice was taped to the front. He'd craved normalcy. Had joined the Army in search of it. While others had chafed at the rules, discipline, and rigid structure, he'd craved them—flourished under them.

He still embraced them.

"Hey." Tristan dragged Shane forward and into a brief, back-slapping hug, which Shane returned. "I haven't seen you in a while. What's up? Everything okay at the firm?"

"Yeah," Shane said, returning the friendly pound. "We're good."

Releasing him, Tristan ran his dark green gaze over Shane's face. "As good as it is to see you, somehow I doubt this is a how-the-hell-are-you? visit. What's up?"

"Jonah Michaels," Shane stated, getting right to the point. He didn't have time to beat around the bush. In the hour since he'd followed Fallon to her job and left her under Maddox's watchful eye, a relentless itch had settled between his shoulder blades. The sense of urgency hadn't abated but had grown more insistent. He couldn't explain the feeling, but he didn't question it, either. It'd saved his ass too often to count both in Afghanistan and on the job here in Boston.

A frown creased Tristan's brow. "Jonah Michaels," he repeated. His eyes narrowed. "Why are you asking me about him? What do you know?"

"I know a couple of his boys nearly killed Fallon last night."

A cold mask dropped over his friend's features, and in that instant, he transformed from best friend to hardened cop. "Where?" he quietly demanded.

"Her apartment. They were lying in wait for her to arrive home." Shane relayed what'd occurred the night before.

"Shit. Where are these two now? Why didn't you call the police?" Tristan snapped.

"Because we handled it." A small, nasty smile curved his lips as he recalled the early morning phone call from Ciaran and Khalil.

After some…persuasion, the two assholes had spilled everything they knew. Which admittedly, hadn't been much. Low in the pecking order, they'd been told to take care of Fallon and make it seem like a mugging gone bad. Nothing more. Shane silently snorted. That assignment had been an epic fail, and in a couple of hours, those two would find themselves with room and board courtesy of the Boston PD.

"You. Handled. It," Tristan bit out. "You had no business 'handling it.' You're not the cops. Are they alive?"

"They're alive." Damn, he was the second person to ask

him that. What? Did he and Fallon believe he'd devolved into a bloodthirsty savage? He snorted. "All we did was transport them to a secure location to ask them some questions."

"And?" Tristan pressed.

"And nothing." Truth. The two thugs were low-level gang members following orders and hoping to gain more status by killing the woman responsible for their leader being locked up. Shane cocked his head, a burgeoning anger simmering in his chest and rising like the mercury in a thermometer. "You don't seem surprised to hear Michaels's and Fallon's names linked. Why is that?" he asked, his tone as deadly soft as Tristan's.

A pause. "Because I'm the lead detective on the case."

You can't punch him. You can't punch him. He's not just your friend but the police. Screw it. Shane crowded into Tristan's personal space, his chest bumping the other man's. "You mean to tell me you've known all along that Fallon was in danger, and you didn't think to mention it to me?"

"Back off," Tristan snarled, fire leaping in his eyes. "We offered to place her in a safe house, but she refused. And since Michaels was locked up and her identity kept under wraps, we didn't force the issue. Besides, you know damn well I couldn't tell you. It was—*is*—a police matter. Only a few of us were aware of her name, and the fewer people, the better chance she remained anonymous."

Logic didn't cool the rage seething inside him. "Well, that ship has not only sailed but been blown to hell and back. Still, it begs the question," Shane continued, unease skulking through his veins and sending the itch between his shoulders into a full-out rash, "why are you being so forthcoming now when you've been close-lipped for the past three months?"

Tristan shifted back a couple a steps and dragged a hand over his short, auburn hair, glancing over his shoulder as if ensuring no one overheard him. "Because Jonah Michaels escaped from our custody this morning."

Unease blazed into razor-edged panic. It sliced into him, sharp, terrifying. Escaped? How? *Jesus Christ*. Inhaling deeply, he buried the alarm beneath a slab of ice. "What happened?"

Fury suffused his friend's face, tightening his mouth into a grim, flat line. "He had a court appearance this morning to set a trial date. On the transfer in, the prison bus was hijacked, and Michaels escaped. A corrections officer was killed, as well as the driver. I just returned from the scene not too long ago. Fallon needs to know. With him on the loose and his gang crazy enough to attack a prison bus, she has to go into witness protection. If her identity has been leaked, killing her will be his first order of business."

"Witness protection? Your department couldn't even protect her name, and now you expect me to entrust her life into that same care?" He shook his head. "No. I—GDG—will guard her."

A part of him conceded his accusation was unfair. The program didn't claim to be infallible, but it worked way more often than it failed. Yet, that small percentage existed, and he wasn't willing to take the chance of Fallon beating the odds. He'd observed firsthand the devastation that it going wrong had wreaked. Five years ago, Ciaran had convinced an associate of one of the most vicious crime families in the country to testify and enter witness protection. Someone had leaked the location, and while trying to rescue the informant, he'd been shot and the informant killed. Ciaran carried the enormous guilt to this day.

An image of Fallon jerking awake from a nightmare, her gray eyes nearly black and sightless with terror, slid across his mind's eye. No, he couldn't bear the possibility of Fallon ending up as a statistic. Not on his watch. And not if he could prevent it.

"I repeat," Tristan ground out. "This is a police matter. Now, since you were sitting on her last night, I'm assuming you know where she is right now." At Shane's silence, Tristan moved forward, reclaiming the space he'd placed between them. "Shane, you are my best friend, but I swear to God I will haul your ass into that station and have you brought up on obstruction charges. If you care about your sister's friend, you will let me do my job. Now where is she?"

Shane arched an eyebrow, not in the least bit intimidated. "Home," he lied. When Tristan glared at him, mistrust glittering in his eyes, Shane added, "Maddox is with her."

Finally, Tristan nodded, the anger slowly fading from his features. Sympathy and resolve replaced the darker emotion, and a slight twinge of guilt over his deception twisted Shane's stomach. Slight though, and nothing he couldn't deal with if it meant Fallon's safety.

"All right," Tristan said, glancing over his shoulder in the direction of the station. "Thanks for the info. I need to get over there then. And, Shane," he clamped a hand on Shane's shoulder, squeezing it, "I'll keep her safe. I promise."

"Tristan."

They both turned at the sound of the soft, feminine voice. As the willowy, tall blonde in a dark green pantsuit approached them, Shane glanced at Tristan...and snorted. God, please never let him wear that same sappy expression on his face. He was embarrassed for his friend.

"What?" Tristan asked, shooting a look at Shane before switching his attention back to Joy Sanders, his fiancée.

"Nothing." Shane shrugged. "I just always wondered exactly what whipped looked like, and now I know."

"Fuck off," he murmured without heat, affection for his woman softening his green eyes and curving his lips. "Hey, sweetheart."

Joy rose on tiptoe and pressed her mouth to Tristan's, her love for the detective just as obvious. Even after the tame kiss, their eyes remained connected, as if transmitting a secret message only the two of them knew. Shane glanced away, feeling like a damn Peeping Tom.

Shane tried not to envy his friend the love of his fiancée. Joy, a computer programmer at one of the most prestigious software companies in the state, was intelligent, beautiful, and kind. She didn't begrudge Tristan his long hours but supported him, and Shane couldn't help but like and admire her. She was perfect for his friend.

He cleared his throat, and Joy smiled at him, sliding an arm around Tristan's waist.

"Hi, Shane," she greeted. "We missed you at dinner last week."

"I'm sorry. Work came up. But I'll be there next time."

"Good." Joy nodded. "I'm holding you to it. So," she said, tipping her head back and refocusing on Tristan, "are you ready?"

"Damn." Tristan winced. "We were supposed to have an early lunch."

"Supposed?" She arched an eyebrow.

"Yeah, something came up on one of my cases, and I

have to take care of it immediately. I'm sorry."

Joy shook her head. "No worries, honey." She brushed her lips across his jaw. "I understand. Will you be home for dinner?"

"I should. If there's a problem, I'll call ahead."

"Sounds good."

"I'm going to head out, too," Shane interrupted, removing his keys from his pocket. "Nice seeing you again, Joy." He leaned forward and quickly hugged her.

"I'll talk to you later, Shane, okay?" The warning in the question reverberated in the narrowed stare Tristan pinned on him.

"Yeah. Later." Shane nodded and climbed into his SUV, leaving Tristan to walk Joy back to her car.

While his friend was preoccupied with his fiancée, Shane had interference to run.

Chapter Six

"Thank you for dining at The Grease Spot," she recited in a bored tone. "Today's specials are—"

"Fallon, I need you to come with me."

Fallon glanced up from her order pad to meet the piercing turquoise stare and gorgeous, stern face that had become the object of her fantasies and the bane of her existence. Last night he'd been tender, caring, and this morning he'd reverted back to his usual two-by-four-up-his-ass demeanor. Especially when she'd announced her intention to show up for her morning shift. For a moment, anger had flared in his gaze, and misplaced anticipation and lust had raced through her, thickened her blood. She could imagine that same hard expression stamped on his face while he brought her to a screaming orgasm. But as quickly as the emotion had blazed, Shane had banked it, his eyes shadowed, inscrutable. He'd herded her out the apartment, followed her to work since she'd insisted on driving, and ordered her to stay put before pulling off.

Even with his cold mask firmly in place, she'd sensed his frustration and irritation. He'd probably assumed her insistence stemmed from stubbornness and defiance. But in three months, the future she'd mapped out—working in an event-planning company, gaining experience under her belt, creating connections, launching her own business—had crumbled beneath her feet like a shaky ledge. First, she'd observed a murder. Second, she'd lost her job. Third, she'd fallen into dead-end employment to pay the bills. And now, he appeared on her doorstep—literally—and threatened the independence she'd fought so hard for.

No, he wouldn't understand but just continue to see her decision as another act of impulsive rebellion.

Well, screw it. He might be her best friend's older brother and have known her for over a decade, but he didn't *know* her. Didn't *see* her.

And most importantly, he didn't want to.

Burying the pain and anger, she flicked a hand, forced a nonchalance she was far from feeling. "Hey, big boy, that *Terminator* shit might work with the other girls, but—"

"Jonah Michaels escaped from jail."

Her heart thudded hard, then raced as if trying to trample a hole in her chest. The rapid tattoo filled her head, her ears. Jonah Michaels…escaped…

"Oh Jesus." She sank to the seat across from him, her knees the consistency of hospital Jell-O. "How?" she rasped, her suddenly numb fingers dropping the pen and order pad on the table. "When?"

"This morning." His voice, that deep, sin-wrapped-in-dark-chocolate voice, could've been relaying the elements on the periodic table instead of delivering terrifying news that threatened her life expectancy. His stoic, reserved expression didn't change. "During a prison transfer. The bus was hijacked, most likely by his gang."

"How's that…?" She dragged her fingers through her hair, fisting the curls. "How's that even possible? Things like that only happen in *The Fast and the Furious*, not reality."

For the first time she glimpsed an emotion flicker across his face. It was a slight tightening of his full, sensual lips, but it was there. "Oh, it's possible."

"Oh my God." Fear grew inside her with each breath she took in. Dropping against the booth's back, she rubbed her palms over her arms, the thin, long-sleeved white shirt no match for the cold invading her body. A cold that infiltrated her soul and had been a part of her ever since she'd been in the wrong place at the wrong time.

All because of a goddamn cup of coffee. She hadn't had a latte since.

"There's more," Shane said. Well Christ, the only thing missing was the ominous *dunh-dunh-dunh-dunh*.

"More?" She loosed a brittle laugh. "Well, aren't you just a wealth of good news today?" Shaking her head, she rubbed her eyes, suddenly weary. "What is it?"

"Jonah knows who you are, and he's going to put everything behind coming for you, Fallon. We did some checking. The murder weapon was never recovered. No DNA. No one else stepped up to finger Michaels. You're all the police and DA have. No witness, no case." His voice deepened. "You're in danger."

"The police," she began but petered off at the flint in his blue-green gaze.

"Can put you up in a safe house or a hotel until the trial," he conceded. "Like I said, you're their only eyewitness to the crime, and it's in their best interest to keep you secured. But placing you in custody doesn't mean you'll make it to the trial. Michaels and his crew have already attacked a prison bus and killed the driver and an officer. The same person who leaked your name might not have an issue with betraying the location of a safe house. Fallon, I don't want to scare you. The police are good, but," he leaned forward and covered her hand with his much bigger one, "we're better. Let me keep you safe. Let me protect you."

She stared down at their stacked hands. Heat from his palm radiated over her skin, rivaling the warmth inside the restaurant. Even in spite of the danger hanging over her head like Damocles's sword, she couldn't help but acknowledge this was the first time in seven years that he'd voluntarily touched her. Last night she'd just about begged. How unfair that it came under these circumstances. Or that her breath stuttered in her lungs, her belly clenched, and a dull ache pulsed in her clit.

He was her easy button.

And he didn't want her. She was his younger sister's immature, reckless, and flighty best friend. Nothing more.

And he was a rigid, stoic stickler. He could probably give her orgasms so mind-blowing she'd create a religion to worship them, but still...

Best she stay focused on more important issues—like staying alive.

"But the circumstances are different than three months ago. Wouldn't I have to go with the police?" She slid her hands from under his and tucked them in her lap, ordering her heart to calm down.

"No. You have the choice of accepting witness protection or opting out just like before. I'm not saying they won't do a good job, Fallon. But guarding people, ensuring their safety and security—that's my job. And I'm damn good at it. And unlike the police and DA's office, I have more of a personal investment than making sure you make it to a trial to testify and win a case."

"Right," she drawled, her fists tightening. "Not making Addy cry with my untimely death."

"Don't," he ordered softly but with an underlying and unmistakable hint of steel. "You know damn well this is about more than an obligation or Addy. You're family. Like my little—"

"Sister," she finished. "Yes, I know." And didn't that just slice her into pieces every damn time he said it? As if she needed constant reminders of how he saw her.

"I protect what's mine," he stated, voice flat. Brooking no argument. Or refusal.

"See? Here's the funny thing. I'm *not* yours. I don't care that you consider me family. We're not. And I still have a choice—choices. I'm not powerless in this situation." Maybe if she said it often enough, she would eventually believe it. "And what about a job? Money? The trial date hasn't even been set as far as I know. What, do you expect me to live off you and your *generous* largesse? I'm not a damn charity case. How am I supposed to support myself?"

Shane might believe she was a spoiled rich kid who refused to grow up, but for two years she'd lived on her own, provided for herself. Even after Carolyn had fired her, she'd taken this waitressing job to pay the bills while she looked for another position with an event-planning company. Not once had she allowed her father to step in and rescue her— no matter how many times she'd wanted him to.

"You're talking about things that are trivial when compared to your life," he snapped. "Goddammit, Fallon. For once, think. How can you weigh gathering drink orders against breathing?"

Anger rolled through her like a barrel of storm clouds. Heat flooded her face, prickled her palms. He didn't get it; he thought she was being silly, fickle Fallon. But of course he did, because Shane couldn't separate the girl from the woman. He couldn't comprehend that her concern was less about the job and more about being a burden, a sycophant who took, took, took and had nothing redeeming to give or offer.

"You're so right," she bit out. "That's exactly what I'm worried about. Enough tips to buy the latest pair of Gucci sunglasses. But how about you humor me and tell me anyway about how I'm supposed to support myself if I'm locked away for months on end."

His sigh could've been one of apology or frustration. Hard to tell since his hooded gaze revealed nothing. "We have the resources to take care of you."

"I don't want to be 'taken care of,'" she snapped, seconds away from slamming her fist on the tabletop. But that action would reinforce his spoiled brat image of her, and she refused to hand him the ammo. "If I agree to this—and I'm stressing *if*—I need to talk with the police first. Then I insist on reimbursing you and your company after the trial is over. That's a condition I'm not budging on." She was no longer that girl dependent on her parents' wealth, and she refused to allow anyone—even a sociopath murderer—to reduce her to that again.

Surprise that he wasn't fast enough to hide flickered in Shane's eyes. He studied her for several long moments almost as if trying to figure out her angle. Well, gee, color her offended.

"Fine." The quiet statement stole the righteous wind out of her sails. Well, damn. She was spoiling for a fight. With the rage, fear, and uncertainty twisting inside her like Dorothy's cyclone, she needed an outlet. Needed a release to calm the storm inside her. "I need to go let my supervisor know I'm leaving, and then we can head for the police station."

"Dammit, Fallon, we don't have time—"

"One," she growled, slipping out of the booth. "My name is not Dammit Fallon or Goddammit Fallon. Two, I'm going to the police. I want to speak with them about Michaels, his escape, and hear their advice on where I should go from here. You can come with me or meet me there."

A beat of silence. "I'm coming with you. No way am I letting you out of my sight," he stated, voice flat. But a tic along his jaw betrayed the emotion hidden under the ice in his tone.

She widened her eyes and batted her lashes until she probably resembled a deranged Betty Boop. "Well now, that's a switch isn't it? Used to be you couldn't wait to get away from me. Now we're bosom buddies."

Not waiting on his response—which would undoubtedly be more stoic, self-suffering silence—she spun around and headed for the kitchen. Ten minutes later, she returned to the dining area sans apron, pen, and order pad, leaving a pissed-off supervisor behind. She sighed. Join the club of people who weren't happy with her at the moment. And the man glaring at her near the front door with a phone pressed to his ear was the lifelong charter member.

"Yeah," he said to the person on the other end. "We're coming out." Pause. "Police station first, then we'll decide from there." Another pause. "Copy that." He ended his call, but the scowl remained firmly in place. "You ready?" he growled.

"Yes."

Silently, he held the door open, allowing her to step out of the restaurant. She sucked in a breath and held it as he pressed in close behind her. *Damn.* Too late. His scent—that unique combination of fresh wind, and skin—teased her nose, setting off a chain reaction of heat, heart palpitations, and flocks of birds in her stomach. She gritted her teeth against the Pavlovian response.

He shifted beside her, his strong, firm upper arm nudging her shoulder. His unblinking, sharp gaze scanned the street and sidewalks as he settled a hand on the small of her back and guided her to the blue BMW convertible parked around the corner. Relief poured through her like a cold drink of water on a hot day. As silly as it seemed, FiFi represented the only stability in her world. The only thing that hadn't meta-morphosed into something unrecognizable or scary.

"You have your key?" Shane didn't glance down at her, his restless survey of their surroundings continuing.

"Yes." She pointed her key fob at the car. The fob had been a gift from her father months ago after he discovered what happened. He'd sent the dealer to her home with the new electronic device, not wanting her to waste seconds opening the car with a key if someone was after her. The gesture had brought tears to her eyes. Though her father had been an absent parent, a preoccupied, distracted one, she'd never doubted he'd loved her. She just wasn't a priority.

Several feet away, she pressed the open button, and the headlights blinked once, the horn beeping twice.

"I'll follow you—"

Shane's words were swallowed by the huge, deafening *boom* from the end of the street. A fiery blast knocked both of them off their feet. Twisting midair, he wrapped his arms and body around her. His back slammed to the concrete hard enough for him to groan in pain. But immediately, he rolled, covering her from head to toe from the heat searing the air around them.

Oh *Jesus*. Jesus, Mary, and Joseph.

FiFi.

Gone. Someone had bombed her beloved FiFi to hell and back.

She blinked, tears burning her eyes as hot as the flames licking at her car.

"—okay?"

She frowned, the ringing in her ears loud and subsiding slowly.

"Are you okay?" Shane repeated, his voice urgent, harsh. The cold reserve had disappeared, melted by the bomb and rage blazing in his eyes. Fury hardened his features, the sculpted cheekbones, angular jaw, and carnal curves of his mouth even more pronounced under his taut skin.

"Y-yes," she stuttered. Then lifted her head and peered over his shoulder at the flaming heap that used to be her darling FiFi. She lowered her head, stared up at the sky, and let the tears fall.

"So where did you say your safe house was?"

Chapter Seven

"This is so…normal."

Shane glanced around the living room of his Cambridge home, trying to see it through Fallon's eyes. Two years ago, he'd taken one look at the three-story, single-family home and had claimed it. White with black shutters and a black iron gate, it'd reminded him of Ebenezer Scrooge's nephew Fred's home in Shane's favorite movie, *A Christmas Carol*. Most people enjoyed the glimpses into Scrooge's past, present, and future. But for him, the scene where Scrooge visited his nephew's home with the Ghost of Christmas Present as well as the end where the former miser came to Fred and his wife and was welcomed into their arms—he'd stayed glued to the television for those moments. Because Fred's home had meant warmth, love, fun, security…family.

Family.

With its exposed beams, maple hardwood floors, stained cabinetry, open floor plan, big rooms, and large fireplaces, this house meant a wife, children—a future. This house meant a place of safety that no one could rip away from him. He would always have food in the stainless-steel refrigerator. When he flicked the wall switch, light would always flood the rooms.

Shane's fantasy had been stability. And purchasing this Cambridge home had been the start of obtaining it.

"What were you expecting?" he asked Fallon, setting the alarm. "Barracks?"

When she didn't reply, he glanced over his shoulder. Fallon perched on the arm of his brown leather sofa, staring straight ahead, her arms wrapped around herself. Alone. He paused. She seemed so alone and a wraith of her usual vibrant self. In that moment, a murderous rage filled him like a seething volcano. For Jonah Michaels. For the coward gang members that followed him like blind disciples. Shane had faced terrorists in battle on the foreign sands of the desert. He'd willingly served his country to protect the liberty and rights of United States citizens. But this—this campaign of terror waged against an innocent woman in the city, the home where she should've felt the safest—was more personal.

Yeah, he could easily kill for her.

"Fallon?"

Her head jerked in his direction. "Yes? I'm sorry. Did you say something?" Heaving a sigh, she shot to her feet and restlessly paced to the dark fireplace. "I'm sorry," she repeated. "I'm just so—"

"Shell-shocked. Scared. Mad as hell," he supplied, heading toward the back door to check the lock.

A snort reached him as he strode down the hallway. "D,

all of the above."

After verifying the security system he'd had installed was operational and pulling the shades on all the windows, he returned to the living room to find Fallon still standing in front of the fireplace, staring into its cold depths.

"Fallon."

"Sometimes I wonder if I'm ever going to be safe again," she whispered. "If Michaels doesn't get to me before the trial, what about after? Will he or his gang leave me alone? Will they want revenge for my testifying?" She emitted an awful sound caught somewhere between a sob and a bark of laughter. "I remember when my biggest worry was whether or not my ass would get pinched at work."

He frowned. *Her ass pinched?* What the— *Focus.* He had to focus on this current situation. Afterward he'd get a name. And break a hand.

Crossing the room, he trained his gaze on the honey-and-cinnamon tangle of curls that begged for a man to stroke, caress…grip. How many times had he envisioned himself tangling his fingers in her hair and jerking her head back to expose that elegant neck as he thrust deep into a pussy that would probably feel like heaven and hell? Pleasure and pain. If he closed his eyes, he could feel the phantom clutch and ripple of her core over his cock. Could groan at the sweet suction that would demand his seed and his soul.

He inhaled, and the hand that reached for her arm trembled slightly. Balling his fingers into a fist, he lowered his arm to his side. But damned himself by moving closer and not stopping until his chest nearly brushed her spine. Her scent drifted up to him, tantalized him as it had the night before when he'd cradled her on his lap.

"What about my parents? Addy? If the Lords of War can't get to me, will they go after the people I love?"

"We already have security details guarding them. Your mother is out of the country, so she should be fine. But your father and Addy, we have them covered." Closing his eyes, he bent his head, his lips hovering near her ear. "What did I promise you?" he asked, the control he wielded to refrain from touching her evident in the hoarse tone of his voice. "Tell me, Fallon."

"That I was safe with you," she finally replied after a long hesitation. Which grated over his skin like sandpaper. There shouldn't be any uncertainty. He'd give his life for her as quickly and easily as he would for Addisyn or his mother. Why didn't she trust in that? *Could be because you've avoided her like an industrial accident since the night she kissed you*, his conscience snidely reminded him. Since arguing with himself smacked too much of bat-shit crazy, he conceded the point. But what was the alternative? Confess the truth? *Fallon, you're my Achilles' heel. I want to fuck you senseless, until you feel me imprinted on you even when I'm not inside you. But that's all I want—all I can allow myself.*

Not only did that sound like a pretentious douche, but it made him a grade-A dick.

"Turn around," he ordered, and waited as she obeyed. For once. She must be in shock. Her soft, troubled gaze met his, and he clenched his fingers until they ached in protest. But he welcomed the dull throb. It reminded him that smoothing the shadowed circles under her eyes was lunacy. Touching her in any capacity would be the height of stupidity. Especially with the image of her back arching, her ass high in the air as she took his cock wavering in his mind like a taunting red flag.

"I know you're frightened, and it seems like everything familiar has disappeared. That nothing will ever be the same again. You feel alone," he murmured, and surrendered to the clawing need to caress her, even if it was a tawny strand of hair that fell over her shoulder. Her breath caught, whether at his words or his clasp of a curl, he couldn't decipher. "I won't leave you."

The doubt that had been in her voice flickered in her eyes. And a fierce longing to command her belief in him, surged hot and swift. He gritted his teeth against the power of it. Then a thought infiltrated the demanding need. How many people, including her parents, had promised the same thing? Even he had pushed her away. Could he blame her for possessing misgivings about his vow to remain by her side? *Damnit, yes.* When it came to her life? Goddamn right he could blame her.

"I'm sorry," she said, the apology a gentle affront to his ears, his pride.

"What do you have to be sorry about?" he asked, softening the hard edge to the question. "Explain."

She shrugged a shoulder, her gaze shifting to some engrossing object over his shoulder. "That Addy dragged you into this mess. It's bad enough my life has gone to hell in gasoline drawers, but I wouldn't have asked you to join in on the ride. It's—I'm—not your responsibility."

"That's just it, Fallon," he said. "Addy shouldn't have had to drag me into anything, and you should have asked. I've willingly placed my life on the line in Afghanistan for U.S. citizens I don't even know. I do it now for clients who pay for my services. For you…" For her, who he'd watched grow from a beautiful girl to a stunning woman. Who he'd protected along with his sister. Who he'd secretly hungered for... For her he would raze Boston to the ground to keep safe. "How could you believe I would do anything less for you?"

A small, tight smile quirked a corner of her mouth. "Of course. Duty." Before he could argue, she backed up, thrusting a hand through her hair and tugging the thick spirals away from her face. "This may be difficult for you to imagine, but I've provided for myself these last two years. I haven't depended on anyone, taken from anyone. I'm not a parasite." She twisted her fingers in front of her, then as if realizing the telltale agitated gesture, dropped her hands and tilted her chin up. "How long? You didn't answer before, but this could stretch out for months. How long are you supposed to put your life on hold for me? Maybe you can assign someone else to protect me? Or I can ask Dad to hire another security firm—"

"Hell. No," he gritted out. "No one takes over. I said I'm not leaving, and I meant it. And as far as how long? Until."

Again, she released a sigh, heavy with irritation. "You can't just—"

"Un. Til." If she believed he would hand her off like a football, he needed to find out what The Grease Spot served in its coffee. Because she'd obviously been drinking too much of it. "Now, are you hungry?"

A long pause. "Sure. Why not? I just need a moment..." She briefly squeezed her eyes shut. "Where's your bathroom?"

"Down the hall to your left. Second door on the left," he instructed. She nodded and whirled around, but not fast enough to conceal the bright sheen in her eyes. The sight of that unexpected moisture grabbed him by the throat and shook. Everything in him demanded he follow her, comfort her, wipe away her tears. But he remained in place, rigid with a screaming tension that hummed in his veins.

His phone vibrated against his hip. Still studying the corridor Fallon had disappeared down, he removed his cell from his pocket. This call had only been a matter of time. "Roarke."

"You bastard," Detective Tristan Scott's deep, furious voice rumbled in Shane's ear.

"Hello to you, too," he said wryly.

"I should have you arrested right goddamn now," his friend snapped. "Obstruction of justice. Tampering with a witness. Being a lying, interfering son of a bitch."

"They have a charge for that?" Shane drawled.

"Cute. Very cute." Tristan paused, and Shane could picture his friend pinching the bridge of his nose, a gesture that telegraphed his struggle to wrestle his temper under control. "You sent me on a wild-goose chase this morning on purpose. You damn well knew Fallon wasn't at her apartment. Then, while that particular gem was dawning on me, I receive a call that a car has been bombed in Allston. And the owner of the car—a witness in a major criminal case—is in the wind. From the statements of bystanders, she left with a tall, dark-haired man. You know what, Shane, I happen to be a detective, and it didn't require Sherlock-level deductions to realize the 'tall, dark-haired man' who lied to me about her location so he could get to her first is probably the same 'tall, dark-haired man' who hauled her away from the scene before police could question her."

With one last scan of the empty hallway, Shane headed

toward the kitchen. "Fallon has decided against entering witness protection and has agreed to let GDG protect her. It's her decision."

"Because you convinced her," Tristan barked.

"Because the police leaked her name and allowed a killer to escape jail. Because two assholes showed up at her home with the intent of blowing her away. Because she was seconds away from being incinerated in the fireball that used to be her car," Shane shot back, anger rising with every point. He jerked the refrigerator door open and glared into the sparse interior. The cool air puffing against his skin did nothing to chill the fire circulating inside his chest. "You're damn right I didn't leave her at the scene. I didn't know if the person who'd FUBAR-ed her car was still there, waiting around to finish off what the bomb hadn't accomplished. This is Fallon, Shane. Twice she's avoided ending up in a morgue with a toe tag. I wasn't going to risk a possible third time being the fucking charm."

A thick, heavy silence descended over the phone line.

"Where is she?" Tristan asked quietly.

"Safe," Shane stated. "With me."

"I'm on my way over there to take her statement."

"No," Shane objected, voice sharp. "You're the lead detective on this case. With Fallon disappearing, who do you think Michaels will have followed? Right now, he doesn't know my identity or her connection to me. I'd like to keep it that way. Besides, we won't be here long anyway. Tomorrow, I'm moving her to one of our safe houses."

Since GDG Security Solutions was a young company compared to other security firms, they only owned three locations. But the one Shane had in mind granted enough distance between Boston, the Lords of War, and Fallon that he could breathe somewhat easier...somewhat.

"I'm trying to be patient, Shane. I really am. But my captain isn't going to be nearly as understanding. One of the most notorious gang leaders in the city busted out of jail, and now the star witness is gone. This doesn't make the department look good." Tristan's sigh echoed down the line. "I get it, man. I do. Fallon is special to you. If this was Joy, I would tear down hell itself to keep her safe." Shane believed him; Tristan was crazy about his fiancée, and would give his life—and take someone else's—to protect her. "But I have a job to do, too," Tristan continued. "And a public to keep safe. Michaels and his boys don't give a rat's ass who they hurt or kill. My hands are tied if Fallon opts out of witness protection, but I can still work on arrests for the car bombing, for the threats on a witness's life."

Shane nodded, though Tristan couldn't see the gesture. "I'll have her call you. I promise. After tonight, I can't reveal where we're headed, but I will keep you in the loop as much as possible," he conceded. Shane loved Tristan like a brother, but with Fallon's life in the balance, he refused to compromise any further.

"Fine," Tristan agreed, though frustration still colored his tone. "I'll call—Wait." A pause. "Joy just came home. I'll be in contact soon."

The call ended, and Shane lowered the phone from his ear, staring at the dark screen.

"Either you're really hot or extremely conflicted about what to cook," a dry voice drawled from the kitchen entrance.

He glanced up, startled. He'd been so deep in thought, he hadn't even heard Fallon approach. Returning his attention to the refrigerator, he reached in and withdrew a block of cheddar cheese and butter. "The conflict is whether to go with the cheese or the leftover Chinese. Since the takeout has been there since last week, I'm going with grilled cheese sandwiches."

"Sounds good." She entered the large kitchen, tugged a chair from under the large table, and sank down onto the seat. He studied her as he withdrew a pan and pot from under the counter. Though weariness still shadowed her pretty eyes like heavy storm clouds, a determined glint reflected in the gray depths. Her shoulders were straighter, and the hard, grim slant had disappeared from her soft, sensual mouth. Not necessarily a good thing since it conjured images that had his dick leaping like a damn cheerleader. "Who was that on the phone?" She propped an elbow on the table, resting her cheek on her palm.

"Tristan," he said, opening a can of tomato soup and pouring it into the pot. Jealousy twisted in his gut. His friend had been able to protect her while Shane had been kept in the dark. Irrational, since Tristan led the investigation, but dammit, *he* should've been there for her, not his friend. *Christ*. He dropped the first sandwich into the pan. *When did I grow a vagina?* "He's going to call later to get your statement about today and probably last night."

"Okay." Shooting from the chair as if a flame had been lit under the seat, she prowled the large room, tilting her head back to peek at the exposed beams, running her fingertips over the granite counters, examining the spice rack filled with seasonings he couldn't pronounce much less use, but that Addisyn had insisted he needed. "I almost didn't recognize Tristan when I first saw him after the shooting. It's been several years. Are you two still close?"

"Yes." Their friendship might be a little strained for a while after today, but as always, they would get over it.

"Hmm." She arched an eyebrow, leaned against the counter bordering the stove where he worked. "I bet he's pissed at you right about now." Shane grunted, and she laughed. The husky chuckle slid under his shirt and over his skin, caressing him. He flipped the grilled cheese with unnecessary force. "I'll take that as a yes. Where are your plates?"

He gestured to the cabinets to his right. "Bottom shelf."

Within moments bowls and plates filled with steaming tomato soup and hot grilled cheese sandwiches set on the table. Stomach growling, he'd devoured a sandwich and emptied his soup bowl before glancing at Fallon. Half her grilled cheese remained as did most of her soup. She pinched off pieces of the bread and swirled her spoon through the creamy broth.

"Not hungry?" he asked.

Her head popped up, and she offered him a rueful smile, resting the spoon on her plate. "Not really. It's good though," she assured him.

"You need to eat. The food not only builds your strength and gives you energy, but it helps with your clarity," he urged her. "And you've lost weight."

Surprise flickered in her gaze. "Yeah, well having a front-row seat to murder kind of kills the appetite. No pun intended." She cocked her head to the side, her eyes narrowing slightly. "How would you know if I've lost weight? It'd been over a year since we last saw each other before you showed up. Even then you barely looked at or talked to me."

Wiping his hands on a napkin, he leaned back in his chair, studying the speculation in her hooded scrutiny, the hint of a curl at the corner of her mouth, the challenging arch of her dark brown eyebrow. The defiant gesture pumped lust through his veins, poking at the dominant side of him that hungered for her surrender to his touch.

"I noticed," he murmured.

Something dark appeared and vanished in her heavy-lidded contemplation. "Can I ask you a question?" she requested, reclining in her seat, mimicking his pose.

Oh hell. *Can I ask you a question* guaranteed the person on the receiving end wouldn't like the inquiry. The only thing more certain to make a man's balls shrivel in fear was *Can we talk?*

He nodded.

"Did you really hate my kiss?" Her gaze dropped to his mouth, lingered, then lifted to meet his once more. "Or did you actually like it?"

Shock slammed into his chest like a sledgehammer only to be incinerated by a backdraft of searing hunger. He slowly straightened, every pint of blood in his body pouring into his cock. Like it? One taste of her, one suckle of his tongue, and he'd nearly hiked her ass up on his mother's kitchen counter and buried his face between those perfect thighs, desperate to discover if her sex possessed the same rich vanilla flavor of her mouth.

"Like it? No," he said softly, staring at her lush bottom lip and the full, dimpled top one. Her lashes lowered. "I fucking loved it," he growled. "Too much."

Her eyes widened, and her low gasp resounded in the room. A part of him acknowledged admitting the truth was a colossal mistake. What purpose would it serve? Especially when he couldn't—wouldn't—act on it.

Almost a year ago, Chayot Grey, a friend and co-owner of Liberty Security Services, a firm that often contracted GDG employees to assist on their jobs, had almost lost the woman who was now his wife to a deranged stalker. Watching his friend, who'd suffered so much, finally find the love of his life, had ignited a desire inside Shane.

A home. Family. As much of a dinosaur as it made him sound, marriage. For the past few months, he'd dated women, but hadn't found that elusive one who stimulated his brain as well as his body. Still, veering from that purpose to indulge in a casual affair with a woman who was strictly off-limits defined lunacy. Because he had a feeling one time with Fallon wouldn't be enough. But it also wouldn't last. Passion so hot meant it would only burn out quicker—and with more damage. Including his relationship with Addy for fucking her best friend.

You're dumber than two boxes of rocks, his cock sneered. And his brain chose that moment to jump the common sense ship and join his Johnson.

Because, goddamn, she was gorgeous.

Fallon was his siren song: beautiful, so damn hard to resist. But giving in to his hunger—his craving for her—would only end in pain, hurt feelings, and estrangement. No doubt though. It would end.

"Then why did you push me away? Tell me you weren't interested? Treat me like I'm Typhoid Mary?"

He leaned forward, frustration and need sharpening his voice. "What would you have had me do, Fallon? Fuck you during your birthday party—"

"Yes."

The blunt, raw "yes" ricocheted off the walls, gaining volume with each rebound until the word throbbed in his head, his chest, his erection.

"And then what?" he ground out past a throat tight with lust. "Become fuck buddies? Because that's all I had to offer you. Fallon, you're my sister's best friend—"

"But I'm *not* your sister. And who said I wanted more?" She leaned forward, again aping his movements. "You insist on shoving me into this box that makes you comfortable. Makes me less threatening. But what if *I* just wanted to fuck *you*? No strings, no commitments, just sex. Just pleasure. Just you inside me. Filling me. Stretching me. Branding me. What if I just need to be taken?"

Their harsh breathing boomed in the room, expanding and expanding until it seemed to cram every corner and available space. ...*I need to be taken*... As in now, not back then. Lust razed through him, damn near consuming him. All the reasons why he should keep his distance from her, maintain a guard-client relationship, evacuated his head like a storm-threatened city. Damn logic...

"Fallon," he rumbled.

His phone vibrated in his pocket, announcing an incoming call. With a low curse, he removed the cell and glanced at the screen.

Tristan.

Relief and disappointment comingled in his chest. Relief because his friend's timely—or untimely—call had aborted a rash action Shane would no doubt later regret.

And disappointment because of the same reason.

"It's Tristan," he said, extending the phone across the

table. "He's probably calling to take your statement."

Fallon accepted the cell, her gaze fixed on him. Desire, confusion, and another shadowed emotion darkened her eyes—eyes he had to look away from or he'd end up grabbing her from the chair and making sure only the desire remained.

"Answer it," he ordered more harshly than he'd intended. But goddamn, when a man's zipper was tattooing his dick, politeness was a stretch. He waited until she swiped a thumb across the screen and lifted the phone to her ear. Then he jerked to his feet and strode from the kitchen.

And far from the only woman who'd ever chipped away at the control he'd always prided himself on.

The only woman who'd ever made him furious, frustrated, and hard at the same time.

The only woman who'd ever had him running scared.

Chapter Eight

For the second time in as many nights, Fallon stared up at a bedroom ceiling surrounded by deafening silence. Well, deafening except for her own pathetic words circling in her head like a Tilt-A-Whirl on crack.

But what if I just wanted to fuck you? No strings, no commitments, just sex… Just you inside me… What if I just need to be taken?

Fallon groaned, slapping her palms to her flaming face. *Jesus.* How could she have said that to him? Hadn't she humiliated herself enough over Shane in the last twelve years? Yet, one appearance with his Terminator come-with-me-if-you-want-to-live routine, and she was practically throwing her pitifully wet thong at him.

Like it? No, I fucking loved it. Too much.

It'd been his shocking, almost brutal admission that had punched her one-way ticket to Cray-cray-ville. After the day she'd had—waking up alone after falling asleep next to

Shane, informed the murderer she was set to testify against had escaped custody, almost being fireballed to death with FiFi, whisked away to Shane's home—she'd been desperate to forget. To dwell on something other than her short life expectancy. Expecting his usual silence or one-word replies to her more outlandish questions, he'd blown her away like her FiFi...

Un-unh. Too soon.

She heaved a sigh, rolled to her side, and switched her obsessive staring to the wall.

Still, pathetic mortification aside, she'd been honest.

From the moment she'd met Shane at thirteen years old, she'd sensed the steely core of honor inside him. Later, as a soldier, he endangered his life and safety every day for the citizens of their country, and now with his company, he did so again. He hadn't needed to promise her he would protect her—it was what he did. What he'd been created for. That honor, integrity, steadfastness had drawn her to him. Well those and the utter hotness that was Shane Roarke.

Yet, he wasn't for her.

He desired the whole shebang. Marriage. A family. A Ward-and-June-Cleaver existence she recognized was an utter lie.

Growing up with her parents, she'd had box seats to the disaster of marriage. Especially when one person loved more than the other. The damage it wreaked on the children was—irrevocable. Fallon no longer flitted from man to man like she used to, but that didn't mean she was on the search for Mr. Right who would walk her down a flower-strewn aisle. She'd ceased that destructive behavior out of love for herself, not because she wanted marriage. "Love for herself" entailed breaking the man-eater cycle her mother had started. It included owning her own business, being financially and emotionally independent, and finally, *finally*, proving she wasn't a replica of her mother.

Not that any of that mattered a tinker's damn. Except for the one admission that sounded as if it'd been dragged through a field of broken glass and abraded with sandpaper, Shane had never minced words with how he felt about her.

In his mind, they had no future. And if she gave herself a reality check, she knew deep down that he was right.

"I need a drink," she muttered. And not tea unless it contained a shot of something hard and eighty proof. Surely even Shane had something to take the edge off stashed in his nearly empty kitchen. Or maybe he had a couple of bottles in the den she'd glimpsed earlier. Only one way to find out. She flung the covers aside and scooted out of bed.

Tugging down the T-shirt that would fit Shane's large frame but dwarfed her more petite one, she slid soundlessly across the hardwood floors on bare feet and exited the guest bedroom. Complete silence wrapped around her like suffocating bubble wrap.

In her apartment, nighttime traffic, the raised voices of late partygoers, and muffled music had always lulled her to sleep. Here, the silence heightened the sense of loneliness and isolation. Even though Shane slept a couple of rooms away.

Shane. In bed. Did he sleep naked or in the boxer briefs he'd worn at her apartment? Did he hog the entire bed or confine himself to one side? If so, which side? She grimaced. Now she couldn't purge the image of a naked Shane sprawled across his mattress, sheets tangled around his lean waist. Great.

She neared the staircase, but paused. Was he awake? When she'd hid—*retired*, not hid, *retired*—to her bedroom earlier, he'd disappeared into the den off the living room. Had he come upstairs yet?

Before she could convince herself seeking him out in the middle of the night was a bad idea, she continued down the hallway. The last door on the right stood ajar. Shane's room. Easing closer, she strained to hear over her thundering heartbeat. No sound escaped the open door to spill out into the hallway. He was probably asleep. And the possibility of vodka was calling her name. Still…

Pressing her palm to the door, she pushed it open, widening the crack a fraction.

Holy shit.

Pearlescent moonlight streamed into the room through the windows, cascading across the floor and the rumpled sheets…

Across the bare chest and thrusting hips of the straining male who fisted and pumped his cock.

God he was beautiful.

Black sweatpants covered his long legs and most of his hips, shoved down far enough to bare taut skin and the delicious cut of his hip bone. Ridged abs were etched in stark relief as he drove into the tight grip of his fist. *Damn.* She swept her tongue over suddenly dry lips. She'd guessed the night before that the bulge beneath his briefs hinted at an impressive erection. But, good God, seeing was believing. He. Was. Huge. Each stroke over his stiff cock required use of his arm, not just his wrist.

Desire and greedy lust poured through her, stiffening her nipples into diamond-hard points and pooling between her thighs, until her sex spasmed with an empty ache. Flames licked over her skin, and beads of sweat dotted her palms and chest.

That should be her hand working his dick with an almost punishing hold. Her fingers sliding his stretched skin back and forth over the bulbous cockhead. Her touch causing him to arch and groan in raw abandon.

Reluctantly, she drew her fascinated gaze away from his hips and traveled up his torso to his face. Her breath snagged in her throat. If she'd thought him beautiful before, the tortured pleasure twisting his features transformed him into something that defied description. The tendons in his neck stood out as his head pressed into the pillow. Though thick lashes hid his eyes, erotic hunger stamped his face in the skin pulled tight over his sharp cheekbones and his lips drawn back in a sensual snarl.

What was he thinking about...*who* was he thinking about? Irrational jealousy flared inside her chest for the woman he imagined fucking. Was it a tall, slender blonde? A petite, slim brunette? Anyone but someone with her light brown, unruly curls and curves.

His hand sped up, and the rasp of his breathing roughened. She stared, captivated, as he drove in and out of his fingers, faster and harder. Her nails dug into her palms as she fought to remain hidden in the shadowed doorway instead of crossing the room, climbing on the bed, palming his cock, and finishing the job.

"Fallon."

I'm busted. I'm so freaking busted. Shock and fear gripped and shook her like a rag doll. How had he known she was standing there? And what would he do now? Yell at her? Berate her… Invite her in, replace her hand with his? Push her head toward that straining, beautiful, hard flesh to impale her mouth? Oh damn. But her feet remained glued to the floor as a wondrous, knee-liquefying thought crashed against her skull.

He doesn't know I'm here. And he'd growled her name. *Her* name. Was he fantasizing about her while bringing himself to pleasure? The possibility shot a spiral of blistering heat through her, culminating in a swirling pool of fire between her legs. What was he imagining? Her vivid, and obviously very nasty, imagination supplied a variety of answers. Her sucking him deep into her mouth. Her riding him to oblivion. Or maybe his mouth on her while she returned the favor at the same time?

Cream spilled from between her folds, dampening her panties as her clit swelled and pulsed in favor of option number three. What should she do now? Leave—hightail it out of there before he realized he had an audience of one? Or stay. Enter that room, climb up on the bed, and turn fantasy into reality.

Her heart lodged in her throat, her stomach clenching in sharp need, anticipation, and fear. What if she went to him and he rejected her…again? The idea of sleeping in his SUV for the foreseeable future didn't sit well with her. But if he turned her away with a harsh "Not interested" like before, his vehicle's backseat would be her new home, because she wouldn't be able to stay in the same house with him.

Another long, low moan rumbled in his chest, reverberating in her belly, stroking over the hypersensitive flesh between her thighs.

She moved into the room.

No thinking. No second-guessing. Her bare feet slid noiselessly across the hardwood floor. But she must've made a sound because his thick lashes lifted, and turquoise fire blazed bright in the shadowed darkness.

Pulling up short at the foot of his bed, she met his hard, luminescent stare. His chest rose and fell on deep, rough breaths. The harsh stamp of arousal on his face didn't ease. The sexual, almost cruel slant of his mouth didn't soften. He didn't beckon her closer.

But he didn't order her out either.

Clutching that small detail like a lifeline, she raised one knee onto the mattress. Then the other. Slowly, she crawled the short distance to his big body, granting him time and opportunity to send her away. Yet, even when she knelt between his spread, hard thighs, he remained silent.

Need was a living animal writhing inside her as she gripped his cock directly above his fist. Hot. Steel. Velvet. She tightened her hold, and it bucked and pulsed in her hand. This close his fresh wind scent was sharper, distilled, and combined with the unique musk that belonged solely to him, it made her mouth water for a taste. A taste…hell. She wanted to gorge herself on him.

His fingers unraveled from his rigid flesh, and as she gave the shaft one lush pump, those long digits speared through her hair, twisting, pulling. Tugging her down to the cock she dreamed about and craved.

Sighing, she rubbed her lips across the cap, her mouth coming away wet with the precum slicking the swollen tip. She hummed, licking the essence of his desire. Sharp. A sweet tartness. And him. Hungering for more, she swiped her tongue over the shallow slit and was rewarded with another pulse of fluid.

Growling, Shane thrust his other hand into her hair, pressing his fingertips to her scalp. Wordlessly, he ordered her to take him. Suck him.

And she obeyed.

Her lips parted over his flesh, swallowed him. A ragged moan ripped the air. His. Hers. Theirs. Because as his thick shaft slid over her tongue, pleasure coursed through her like rushing waters bursting free from a dam. God, he was hard, wide…delicious. She curled her tongue under the flared hood of the head and gave a healthy suck.

His dark growl preceded the tiny pricks of pain to her scalp as he yanked on her hair. Those bee stings reverberated in her clit, sparking and aching in correspondence with each tug. Needing more, yearning for more, she rose slightly, angling her head. At this new position she took him deeper, engulfed almost half of his cock. Groaning, she reveled in the stretch of her lips, the pulse beneath his taut skin, the strain in his thighs.

"Don't play with me, Fallon," Shane snarled with another pull on her curls. "You came in here for something. Take it. Suck it." He rolled his hips, pushing another inch into her mouth. "Suck it hard, baby."

The raw eroticism and demand in the words enflamed her. Her pussy clenched, and if she'd had a free hand, she would've touched herself to alleviate the ache. But with both hands around his cock, she wasn't letting go. Not yet. Not until he flooded her mouth and throat.

She withdrew, dragging her mouth and tongue up his dick at a slow, leisurely pace, pausing to swirl her tongue around the swollen head, before descending down, down until her lips bumped her fist. God, she could come from this. This wasn't her first rodeo with a blow job, but she'd never understood the lure of it. How a woman received pleasure from it. But now she did. With every wrench on her hair, every muttered curse, every jerk of his flesh, she understood. Because his desire fed hers. Knowing she made this beautiful male animal tremble tossed kindling on the fire blazing in her core.

Closing her eyes, cheeks hollowed, she rose and fell over his flesh over and over, the wet suction of mouth over skin filling the room like a sexual symphony. She lost herself in the sensuous glide of his rigid cock over her tongue, the hoarse breaths and harsh groans, the samples of his cum with every lick to the bulbous tip. Pumping one hand, she lowered the other between his thighs to cup his balls, squeeze and roll them.

"Goddammit," he rasped. "I told you about teasing me," he warned. Tightening his hold on her head, he held her steady, immobile. "Now I'm going to fuck this pretty mouth. Open wide, baby." He barely waited until she acquiesced before thrusting between her lips in a fast, hard pace. That quickly he wrenched the control from her, making her a prisoner to his hunger and lust. And she loved it. Loved every stroke, every pulse, every raw curse.

"Wider. More," he ordered, his hips punching upward in a rhythm echoing in her clit, her pussy. Digging her fingers into his thighs, all she could do was hold on for the ride. "Dammit, more," he growled, and she stretched her mouth wider until the pull resulted in a dull ache. But she didn't ease up, giving him what he asked, demanded.

"Yeah, baby." He groaned. "I'm about to come. Damn,

I'm about to come hard." His hips slowed as he tilted her head back slightly so she could meet his burning gaze without slipping from her mouth. "Out or in?"

In reply, she sucked harder on his cock. And he swore, resuming the rapid thrusts. His shaft swelled, expanding until he seemed to fill and brand every inch of her mouth. Then, with a long, low, rough roar, he stiffened. Exploded. Her name caressed her ears as hot, thick spurts blasted over her tongue, hitting the back of her throat. Eagerly, she swallowed, taking everything he had to give her. His big body bowed, tremors running through him. And still she continued to draw on him, licking, comforting.

As his jagged breathing evened and eventually quieted, she pressed a last gentle kiss to his flesh, scattering small presses of her lips to his hip and thigh. Just moments before the room had been soaked with serrated groans, carnal demands, and hoarse curses. But now, after the storm had crashed and ebbed, the silence rolled in like a dense fog. Bringing with it the cold, the confusion, the dark.

Shivering, and not from the unsated desire that thrummed under her skin and between her legs, Fallon inched off the bed, her gaze on his thighs, on his ridged abdomen, on the cock that still remained long and thick in spite of his recent release.

Anywhere but his face. If she spied greed there, she might not leave the room, or him. But if she spotted the cold reserve there, the rejection, she might go Lorena Bobbitt on him. She couldn't handle that with the taste of him still strong in her mouth. The feel of his dominant thrusts still echoing on her tongue...

A hard, unyielding hand gripped her wrist.

She jerked her head up.

"Where do you think you're going?" Shane's voice, hoarse from his orgasm, danced over her skin, stroked between her legs. He sat, drew her back onto the bed, and flipped her over so he loomed over her. His palms pressed the mattress on either side of her head, his knees nudging her inner thighs. "We're not finished."

Slowly, without breaking the hot connection of their gazes, he lowered until his torso covered hers. No way he could miss the rapid, harsh puffs of breath escaping her lips or the tight points of her nipples poking his chest. As he slid down, her stomach muscles contracted almost to the point of pain. Anticipation. Terrible, delicious anticipation pounded in her blood, clenched her abdomen, quivered in her sex. Part of her brain struggled with the reality of it, certain she was dreaming and any second would wake up, trembling, hot, sweaty, and unsatisfied.

But the cool rush of air tickling her thighs assured her this wasn't a fantasy. Shane was pushing her T-shirt up her legs, baring her shamefully damp flesh to his gaze. Spread wide, she couldn't hide her reaction to him. And the thin panel of her panties might cover her sex, but it most likely wasn't concealing how aroused and wet she was for him.

He knelt between her legs, rising like some unholy god of all things carnal. His narrowed study branded her as he pushed her shirt higher. She shivered, as much from the lust racing through her as the slight, air-conditioned drafts licking across her hips, stomach, and breasts.

"I knew you would be gorgeous," he uttered, his tone gruff, almost reluctant. "And I knew…" He didn't finish, instead dipped his head and captured a taut nipple between his lips.

Her cry bounced off the walls of the room, echoed in her ears. Trembling escalated into full-out quakes as she tunneled her fingers through his hair, held his head close. Her back arched, offering more of herself to his mouth, his tongue. He sucked hard on her flesh, grazing his teeth over the beaded tip, then soothing the sting with greedy licks.

God, it was so good. *He* made her feel so damn good. No one else had ever made her body sing like this.

"Shane." She whimpered, gripped his head harder. "Please," she pleaded.

Mind reading must've been included in his repertoire, because he murmured something low and unintelligible against her breast and trailed his hand down her belly, under the edge of her panties. Just as he lifted his head and treated her neglected breast to the same sweet attention, he drove a finger into her pussy.

Her heels dug into the bed, her hips rising to his touch. Jesus, that blunt, long finger stretched tissue that hadn't seen action in months. She squeezed her thighs together around his hand, trapping him inside her.

"Relax for me, baby," he whispered, kneading her breast and pinching her nipple with his free hand. "Let me in." In spite of her tight clasp, he withdrew and thrust back in with two fingers. With another strangled cry, her legs fell apart. "Damn, you're tight, but so wet." He groaned, and she savored the hungry, dark sound—a sound and need *she* incited within him.

He set up a quick, breath-stealing pace, his knuckles bumping against her swollen folds with each plunge. He was relentless, propelling her toward a cataclysmic release. She could do nothing but twist and writhe under him, a willing prisoner to his mouth and hands who received the pleasure he doled out.

She strained toward him, clutching him close and riding his fingers with a fervor reserved only for the desperate search for orgasm.

"Come hard for me," he softly ordered against her skin. "I want to feel every bit of it. Understand, Fallon?"

Jerking her head, she gasped, unable to voice her acquiescence. Latching on to her breast, he drew hard, pressing the bud against the roof of his mouth with his tongue. And below. Oh Jesus Christ, below he curled his fingertips against a magic button deep and high in her core. God, she was…

She exploded. Soared over the edge into ecstasy so hot she wouldn't have been surprised to find out she'd pulled a Wicked Witch of the West. Low murmurs filled her ear and broad palms stroked down her spine, her side as tremors rippled through her.

Drifting back down, a warm satisfaction weighed down her limbs. Lethargy crept in, but so did the return of that awful silence.

The awful, awkward silence.

This time when she eased off the bed, he didn't stop her. And without a word, she turned and escaped the room, closing the door behind her. Once she reached the guestroom, she climbed back into bed, jerking the sheets over her shoulders. Her soft pants seemed like cannon blasts in the room as her mind replayed what had occurred in his bedroom.

Shit.

If Shane had avoided her for years because of a kiss, he might leave the country over a blow and hand job.

Chapter Nine

Somewhere a village was missing its idiot.

And he stood six three, wore a size fourteen boot, and carried around guilt like a man purse.

Seven years of steering clear of temptation. Seven years of maintaining a stranglehold on his control. Seven years of keeping his hands off.

Then one night with her in his house, and Shane had blown that accomplishment six ways to Sunday.

Dick. One. Sanity. Zero.

The woman could drive a saint to a night of hitting the bourbon. And last time he checked, his halo had been placed on permanent layaway.

Swearing, he jerked a black, long-sleeved T-shirt over his head, then dropped to the bed to pull on his boots. Giving his shoelace a vicious yank, he swore he could still smell her vanilla scent on the sheets. Could still feel the powerful almost bruising clamp of her sex on his fingers. Could still hear the soft suction of her mouth on his cock, feel the vibration up and down his length from the little hum she made in her throat. A hum of pleasure. Of hunger.

What the hell had he been thinking?

That's just it—he hadn't been thinking. At least not with the correct head.

Being in Fallon's company the past two days had been like a sensory overload after years of deprivation. She'd stoked a hunger in him so bright a cold shower hadn't been able to quench the flames. So he'd taken matters into his own hand—literally. He'd lain in bed long after the light under her door had dimmed, and imagined his fist was her tight core squeezing him, milking him. Behind his eyelids, he'd envisioned her naked, golden body, glistening with sweat, rising and falling over him. Her toned, strong thighs caging his hips, her beautiful breasts with their stiff tips grazing his chest. Her head thrown back, her hair, dark brown and damp with moisture, sticking to her shoulders and neck.

The fantasy had him barreling toward orgasm. And as he lay there, fucking his palm, he heard it—a hushed rustle. A soft whisper like clothes brushing against skin. He'd opened his eyes, and his fantasy had come to vivid life. Fallon. Watching him. Hearing him groan her name.

As she'd stood at the foot of his bed, he should've stopped her. Should've ordered her to turn around and leave. Should've exercised the damn discipline he prided himself on.

Instead he'd remained quiet and received a blow job that had damn near placed him on the endangered species list. And nearly drowned in the pleasure of her uninhibited response as he brought her to orgasm. The vision of Fallon caught in the middle of release wavered in front of his eyes. Sexy. Beautiful. Unforgettable.

He wasn't a monk; he enjoyed sex. Loved the musk of it, the groans, sighs, and erotic suction of flesh penetrating flesh. The liquid heat and muscled clasp of a woman's pussy as he burrowed deep inside her. Yeah, he enjoyed sex. But still…since the first time he fucked at fifteen to the last time months ago, none of the encounters—none of the women— compared to Fallon and the need and ecstasy he'd found in having her lips wrapped around his cock or feeling her squeeze him like a vise as she came.

Afterward, as sweat had dried on both of them, and her body ceased to shudder next to him, he'd glimpsed the un- certainty in her eyes. Noted it in the way she'd quietly ex- ited the room. A kinder, more sensitive man would've called her back, held her…something. But he was a weak son of a bitch, and he'd allowed her to go.

Weak because he'd wanted to ask her to stay, to not leave the bed until it was on trembling legs, achy thighs, and a tender pussy. But he couldn't. Touching her, allowing her to touch him, had been a mistake. One he couldn't repeat. Yet, how they could pretend last night hadn't happened— how he could burn the memory from his brain—he had no clue. If he escaped this ordeal with his control intact and his cock firmly tucked in his pants, it would be a minor miracle.

He rose, glanced at the digital clock on his nightstand, and scrubbed rough palms down his face before dragging them over his head. Christ, six a.m. Six hours after she'd left his room, and she still wouldn't leave him alone. Not physically. Mentally, emotionally. Fallon had been a fixture in his mind for so long he should charge her rent.

But between the time he'd looked up to find her in his bedroom and now, the facts hadn't changed. Fallon was his little sister's best friend. She wasn't for him.

Frowning, he swiped his wallet and phone off the bedside table and left the bedroom. A moment later, he descended the steps to the first floor and entered the kitchen.

He jerked to an abrupt stop.

So much for the pep talk.

His cock lurched behind his zipper, stretching and throbbing. He held still, certain if he made one movement, he'd explode like a pimply-faced teenager copping his first illicit glimpse of breasts. Shutting his eyes, he silently swore. But seconds later, he fixed his gaze on the ball-squeezing sight that greeted him.

Fallon, cooking breakfast in a sleeveless white shirt, her breasts thrusting against the thin material, and a pair of jeans that had probably required grease and a prayer to squeeze into. Damn, the way the denim molded to the curves of her ass… And God Almighty, what an ass. His scrutiny dropped to her bare feet with their pink-painted toes. Simple and somehow as sexy as a December centerfold.

If he stayed there in the kitchen with her, he would have her laid out on the table, his face buried between her thighs, her screams and thighs caressing his ears. And he wouldn't stop there. He wouldn't stop until he was lodged so deep inside her, he might not ever find his way out again.

And he might not want to.

Christ, a primitive, possessive part of him *knew* he wouldn't want to. She was the exact antithesis of him. Yet she was the only woman his body raged for.

What a monumental clusterfuck. One he'd placed

himself square in the middle of.

"Cooking?" he asked, cursing the gravel-roughened tone. It could be mistaken for early morning hoarseness, but the erection in his pants called out that lie.

She started, not having noticed him in the doorway. Lifting her head, she met his intent scrutiny, the spatula in her hand suspended over the pan. The memory of the previous night lit her gray gaze, and he clenched his jaw.

Hands off. You're here to protect her, that's it.

The admonition looped in his head like a subliminal tape trying to convince him smoking was bad. At this moment, she presented more of a danger than becoming hooked on nicotine. With a patch and willpower he could kick that habit. Her? There hadn't been a rehab established that could make him forget the addicting feel of her mouth on his dick. Or keep him from craving more.

"I've been out of my mother's house and on my own for years now. It was either learn to cook or live off of Hot Pockets and ramen noodles. Do you want an omelet?"

He shifted out of the doorway and into the kitchen. "Sure, thank you." He scanned her body once more. Gritted his teeth against the further tightening of his body "Where did you get the clothes?"

"I found some of Addy's things in the other spare bedroom. I hope you don't mind. We're about the same size, and I know she wouldn't care."

About the same size. He silently snorted. Yes, she and his sister were both petite but where Addy was slender, Fallon possessed curves that women paid good money to a surgeon to obtain.

"We're leaving here in about an hour. Once we are out

of town, I'll stop so you can pick up some clothes and other items." So stilted, so stiff. And it didn't help he couldn't keep his attention from dropping to her mouth. See if it was swollen from the not so gentle way he'd used it.

"I'll be ready, let me just finish up here." She flipped the egg in the pan with a neat, efficient twist of her wrist he couldn't help but admire. He'd learned to cook for Addisyn, his mother, and himself at an early age—he'd had to. But he'd never mastered the omelet flip. "So," she said, her dense tangle of curls obscuring the side of her face, "are we not going to talk about last night?"

Desire and trepidation knotted his gut. "Fallon—"

Glass exploded.

Shane dove for Fallon, grabbing her around the waist and twisting midair so he received the brunt of the impact to the floor. Immediately, he rolled, covering her with his body, shielding her head with his arms. Shards crashed and splintered against the marble island, the only barrier between them and the lethal glass slivers.

For a moment, the air thickened, shifted, then wavered, transforming into a giant heat wave. The kitchen floor mutated into hard-packed dirt that smeared his face and coated his tongue. The acrid stench of cordite stung his nostrils as chunks of concrete and grit pelted him. Fire and agony ripped through his lower back…

"Shane?" The tremor in Fallon's whisper boomeranged him to the present and out of the hellish past.

"Are you okay?" he barked, lifting his arms and head, already scanning her face and upper body for himself.

"Y-yes," she stammered, eyes wide with terror. "I'm—"

Dull, loud thumps resounded against the walls and

cabinets, accompanied by the shattering of more glass and the staccato blasts of gunfire.

"Fuck!" he barked. Bullets ripped apart the curtains over the sink, destroying the decorative window and more glass rained down. He had to get her out of there.

Crouching over her, he tugged her up, but was careful to remain below the relative safety of the island. Relative because whoever was shooting up the front of his house wouldn't be satisfied with waiting them out.

He darted a glance at her bare feet and the splinters covering the floor. Bending low, he hiked her into his arms and shot across the kitchen and into the bordering hall. A bullet buried into the wall next to his hip as he cleared the doorway. A few more steps and he stopped in front of a hall closet, opened the door, and shoved her inside. For once she didn't object, didn't give him a hard time. And as he shut the door, he carried the image of her pale skin, dark eyes, and trembling mouth with him.

Icy rage filled him. They'd shot up his home. Endangered innocent people. Tried to kill the woman under his protection—the woman he cared for. Of all their crimes, the last one was the most heinous. The one he wanted blood for.

Edging along the wall, he reached the mouth of the corridor and dropped to a crab walk. Gunfire continued to erupt and burst into the living room from the obliterated bay windows, cleaving chunks of wood off the coffee table and ripping apart the couch.

His boots crunched on glass as he scurried to an end table, jerked the drawer open, and removed one of the SIG Sauers he'd stashed around the house. Ducking behind the couch, he checked the clip, paused, waited. Listened.

From the volume of bullets and the rate at which they were shot, he guessed two, possibly three, shooters. Front of the house. With most of the damage inflicted on the living room and some in the kitchen, the sons of bitches were either on the sidewalk right outside his house, or maybe in his yard. But that could change at any moment.

Their job was to kill. Sooner or later they would infiltrate the house to make sure the mission was accomplished.

No way in hell would he allow that to happen.

Snatching an afghan off the arm of the couch, he gave the blanket a violent shake, scattering most of the shards. Satisfied, he balled it up, pressed it against his chest and belly, and laid on the floor. Scooting around the sofa, he swiftly made his way to the window. He shoved the larger pieces of glass aside with his forearms, ignoring the minute pricks to his skin. Hoping his hands would remain dry, free of blood, and steady.

Moments later, he neared the decimated bay window—*bitches*—and jumped to his feet, shoulder pressed to the wall bordering the pane. A quick, furtive glance outside confirmed his suspicions. Two shooters, both in his yard and slowly creeping closer. A dark blue sedan idled in the street, most likely with a driver behind the wheel.

Pulling back the slide, he loaded a round, then raised the SIG, wrapped both hands around the grip, index finger resting along the barrel. Inhaling, he shifted forward, peered down the rear sight...and fired.

The asshole closest to the house dropped his gun, clutched his shoulder with a sharp cry. For a second, the firing ceased, his partner probably stunned by his boy going down. Absorbing the echo of the recoil vibrating up his arm,

Shane grasped immediate advantage and shot again.

"Shit!" The roar boomed in the sudden silence as the other thug grabbed his firing arm, the automatic weapon in his hand tumbling to the ground. The door to the sedan flew open and another man leaped out, running to his friends.

Flattening his mouth into a grim line, Shane balked at shooting an unarmed man even though he'd driven his "brothers" to Shane's house to kill Fallon. Still… Taking aim again, he shot out a rear tire and a front tire. *Try driving away on rims, motherfuckers.*

In the distance, sirens wailed, the shooting probably called in by his neighbors.

Damn it. He glared out the window, gun raised as the three men hobbled down the street and away from the cops closing in. Lowering his SIG, he charged across the living room and into the hall.

Priority number one: get Fallon out and away from the house before the police arrived. The cops would insist on obtaining a statement, which translated into a trip to the station and detainment for God knew how long. It was time they couldn't afford. Time he could use to put distance between her, Jonah Michaels, and the Lords of War. Time that meant life or death. Hers.

He jerked the closet door open. Fallon flew out as if discharged from a cannon.

"Oomph." The impact of her barreling into him drove the air from his lungs. Automatically, his arms rose to lock around her. Relief blasted through him. She was safe. For the moment. "They're gone, baby," he assured her, pressing a brief, hard kiss to her wild curls. "But we have to go before the police arrive. Hurry." Thank God he'd had the foresight to pack a duffel bag the night before and store it in his SUV. "Hold on." Hiking her into his arms, he dashed to the foyer, grabbed his keys, punched in the security code, and rushed out of the house.

In seconds, he pealed out of the driveway and hit the street, speeding in the same direction of the sirens and incoming police. As several patrol cars flew past his truck, he eased off the accelerator. But as soon as they disappeared in his rearview mirror, he floored it.

Urgency pumped through his veins like a drug. Until he hit the city limits, got rid of the SUV, and arrived at the safe house, he would remain on edge.

Unnerved.

As of now, he couldn't trust the cops or law enforcement.

Because outside of Khalil, Maddox, and Ciaran, only one other person had been aware of Fallon's location. Had known Shane intended to move her this morning.

One of Boston's finest.

Tristan.

Chapter Ten

"God, Shane. Your CD collection is from last century."

Shane gritted his teeth against the crinkle of flipping plastic sleeves and Fallon's irritated grumble. They'd been on the road for forty-five minutes. A *long* forty-five minutes. If it didn't mean a possible fiery death by car crash, he would have closed his eyes and counted to ten—or a hundred. Anything to clamp a stranglehold on his patience.

Damn. Bad analogy. Especially when his gut still clenched in terror and rage at the thought of her being incinerated by a car bomb and most recently by an assassination squad. He would never forget the terror on her face. Damn it! His home was supposed to have been a haven for her. Instead it'd been turned into a firing range with her as the paper target.

Six years in the service and three years with GDG had exposed him to several precarious situations. But facing down the enemy on foreign soil or protecting a client from an obsessed stalker hadn't prepared him for the stark horror that darkened her lovely eyes from silver to almost black.

Never. Never again would he allow danger that close to her.

He glanced toward the passenger side, needing to look at her, reassure himself she was unscathed. With a muttered curse, he jerked his attention back to the road.

At some point during this ride he was going to need to figure out how not to stare at her slim thighs in those ri-diculous—sexy—jeans. Christ on the cross. He shifted in his seat, prayed she didn't notice the growing erection along his thigh. Explaining why he sported a hard-on in her presence notched right under shaving his balls and above watching a *Sex in the City* marathon.

He slid another glance across the bucket seat in the large SUV. Those frivolous—gorgeous—curls that had al-ways fascinated him brushed her high cheekbone and jaw as she continued to peruse his binder of music. Except now he knew the silken, sensual feel of them tangled around his fin-gers. And no amount of rubbing could erase the sensation.

His grip on the steering wheel tightened until the ridges dug into his fingers. A dull ache flared in his joints, protesting the punishing hold. Maybe if he squeezed hard enough, his mind would focus on the danger pursuing them instead of her thighs, her wicked mouth, and her absolutely delicious scent permeating the confines of the car.

"Queen? Greatest hits?" She plucked the disc from its pocket and waved it. "For real?"

By the time they reached their destination, he would be breathing enamel from all the teeth grinding. "They're classic."

She snorted, replaced the CD, and once more blessed silence filled the vehicle.

Then she started singing.

He growled, and she broke off mid-"Bohemian Rhapsody," hands shooting up in the age-old sign of surrender. "Fine, fine." She smirked. "But being the big bad security specialist, you miiiight want to bump some Jay Z or slip a couple of 50 Cent CDs in here. I'm just saying."

He shot her a glare, and she shrugged. Moments later, the sultry notes of Alicia Keys's "If I Ain't Got You" streamed from the speakers. He jabbed the forward button at the same time she reached for it. Their fingers bumped in their haste to skip the song that had been playing from the living room when Fallon had cornered him the kitchen those years ago.

Apparently he wasn't the only one who hadn't scrubbed every detail of that kiss from their mind. *Christ, just don't let her ask why I have the CD in the first place.* He didn't have an answer that wouldn't make him look like a schmuck.

She lowered her arm and cleared her throat as the next track played.

"So where are we headed?" she murmured, and he detected the traces of the fear she'd covered with the derision of his musical tastes.

Rage edged in helplessness flowed through him, obliterating all traces of embarrassment. Rage at the killer who would snuff out such a vibrant, beautiful life as easily as he would a cigarette butt. Helplessness because no matter how much Shane assured Fallon nothing would happen to her while under his watch, the subtle, bitter tinge of fear stained her steady, calm voice. He ached to strangle Jonah Michaels for that alone.

"Cape Cod. Eastham."

The location was ideal; in May, tourists would be flocking to the coastal town. Two more would go unnoticed. Especially since he didn't plan on venturing out of the safe house more than necessary—Fallon, not at all. A good part of the houses dotting the shore were rentals and vacant during the week, providing privacy and cover.

Ten minutes later, he exited off I-93 steered the SUV into a supermarket lot, and parked next to a gunmetal Range Rover. The driver's door of the Rover opened, and Ciaran stepped out of the vehicle.

"Wait here for a minute," he said to Fallon. But her hand was already on the handle, tugging on it, and pushing the door open. He sighed and followed.

"Ciaran," she crowed, delight in her voice as she ran to his best friend and threw her arms around his neck. Shane gritted his teeth and fought against the inexplicable primal urge to yank her out of his friend's embrace and back to his side. "It's been forever."

Ciaran grinned, squeezing her hard. "Hey, sweetheart." He twirled a thick curl around his finger and gave the strands a playful tug. "Still right smack in the middle of trouble, I see." He chuckled when she smacked him on the arm, but an instant later his smile faded, his expression sobering. "I don't want you to worry, okay? We have your back and aren't going to let anything happen to you."

"I know." She glanced over her shoulder at Shane before shifting her attention back to Ciaran. "I'm in capable, if musically challenged, hands."

"Jesus Christ," Shane muttered as Ciaran snorted.

"You must've seen his CD collection," Ciaran said. "Chicago, right?"

"Queen, you rat bastard," Shane growled. "Now, give me the keys so we can get out of here."

With a snicker, Ciaran tossed a pair of keys to him. "Fallon, I have a pair of sneakers in the passenger's seat for you." He aimed a pointed look at her bare feet and arched an eyebrow.

"Thanks." She rose on her toes and kissed his cheek, then climbed into the Rover.

Shane waited until the door closed before turning to his friend and business partner. "Thanks for picking up everything for her."

Ciaran shrugged a shoulder. "Thank your sister. If she hadn't *told* me what to buy, I would've shown up with a toothbrush," he said, dumping a load of sarcasm on "told." Shane grunted, he could just imagine how his bossy younger sister had instructed the other man.

"What have you found out?" Shane crossed his arms, glancing down at his watch. 7:20. Only an hour and five minutes had passed since he walked into the kitchen to find Fallon cooking breakfast. Jesus, it felt like days. "Anything on the shooters?"

Ciaran shook his head, his features tightening. "Nothing. I've been listening to the police scanners and, even with descriptions from your neighbors, somehow the cops missed them. They do have the car, though. Good thinking popping those tires."

"They can pull fingerprints from it at least." Shane rubbed a hand over the nape of his neck. "What about the security cameras from the businesses where Fallon's car was parked?" Khalil had been working to retrieve the footage from the stores on that street to see if the cameras had caught images of the ones who'd placed the bomb on the convertible.

"Most of the angles were wrong and didn't catch anything. But the bakery and pawnshop did capture something. About eleven o'clock, a hooded figure paused beside her car. It isn't very clear what he was doing, but he did spend about three minutes there. Just from the limited amount of time he took, the device couldn't have been very sophisticated. Maybe a pressure-cooker bomb or pipe bomb. Either can be detonated with a cell phone or digital watch. I can ask Tristan if they received the bomb squad's report yet—"

"No," Shane said, voice flat. "From now on we keep everything in-house."

"Shane, I know what you said, but—" Ciaran began, frowning. But once more, Shane cut his friend off.

"I get it, Ciaran," he snapped, frustration and the churning in his stomach lending a jagged edge to his tone. "I do. I don't want to believe Tristan could betray us like that." He shook his head. A part of him *refused* to believe it. "But he was the only other person besides us who knew my identity, where I lived, and that Fallon was with me. I can't let friendship blind me to that fact. Not when her life is on the line."

"Yeah, I understand, but…" He scrubbed a palm over his clean-shaven jaw. "He's already calling, wanting to know where you and Fallon are."

"Just tell him I moved her to the safe house and that we'll be in touch."

"Got it." He sighed, resolution tightening his mouth, though his blue gaze remained troubled. "Listen, we have everything covered in Boston. One of us will contact you whether we find something or not. Maddox and some of our guys have been staking out the Lords of War territory and haunts, see if they can spot Michaels. So far he's in the wind, but we're staying on it."

"Add Tristan to that surveillance."

Mouth in a grim line, Ciaran nodded, the gesture terse. "On it. You just take care of our girl."

Dipping his head in acknowledgement, Shane clasped his friend's hand, then tugged him in for a quick, hard hug.

"Be careful," Shane warned gruffly. As an ex-soldier, he longed to be in the middle of the investigation, the battle, hunting his enemy, and neutralizing the threat. But something deeper, more primal overrode that need. The need to protect. To defend his…his… His what?

Friend? Not only had that ship sailed, but it had been blasted to Davy Jones's Locker.

Labels. Goddamn labels. She was his to keep safe.

Fifteen minutes after pulling into the parking lot, Shane guided the gray Range Rover back onto the interstate with Ciaran headed in the opposite direction toward Boston.

An hour later, Shane drove down a private dirt road and parked in a shell driveway behind a beach house. The two stories of white wood, brick, and glass that soared up above the Cape Cod Bay waterfront was an investment they'd made to bring their wealthier clients. But other than comfort, the secluded location of the home was ideal. The nearest neighbor lived a mile down the road, and the dense border of trees provided more privacy. To the rear stretched a long, remote band of beach with its own stairway and the Atlantic Ocean. Isolation aside, the trees worried him. They provided cover if someone wanted to approach the house undetected. But the other two safe house sites were more populated, offering greater risk of Fallon being discovered. So the beach house it was.

Twenty minutes later, he had their small number of belongings stashed in two of the three bedrooms. Walking through the house with Fallon by his side, he ran through a quick tour. Eight rooms with fireplaces in five of them, a deck *and* screened porch, a huge kitchen with decorative bricks on the floor... He shot a glance at Fallon, who stood at one of the living room's floor-to-ceiling windows that granted a view of the light brown shore, endless ocean, and cloudless sky.

This—the luxury and wealth—probably didn't shock her. As a privileged child of Boston's social and financial elite, she'd grown up surrounded by affluence. He wouldn't be surprised to discover her family owned one of the Mc-Mansions that colonized the Cape and surrounding islands. Yet another difference between them—their worlds.

Turning away from the tempting and oddly vulnerable sight of her at the window silhouetted by massive sky and ocean, he exited the room. Khalil had driven up the night before to ensure the pantry and kitchen were fully stocked and prepared so they wouldn't have to venture out too often. Checking their supplies and the security on the home would provide his hands and mind with something to do.

Moments later, Fallon appeared behind him at the front door, his first stop in securing the residence.

"So this is one of your company's safe houses?" she asked, rubbing her arms. He glanced over his shoulder, strong-arming the urge to replace her hands with his own.

Damnit, no. He returned his attention to the double-bolt lock and alarm pad. Touching was strictly prohibited.

Because if he started touching her, he wouldn't stop. That was the bare, raw truth of it. He wouldn't stop until she twisted and moaned beneath him.

Yeah. Looking and/or touching her right now? Bad idea.

"Yes."

"It's nice," she continued in spite of his abrupt reply. "Your firm must be doing really well. Addy said in the three years it's been open, you've had a steady clientele." When he didn't reply, instead forced himself to focus on his task, she continued. "I meant to ask you. Isn't there some sort of policy against you guarding me? Because of the personal connection?"

He set the alarm system, then without sparing her a glance, he strode toward the kitchen and back door.

"If I was a police officer, probably. But I'm an owner in the company. And you're like family," he said, frowning at the simple knob lock. A well-placed shoulder and enough force would bust the door wide open. He'd have to fortify it. "Your safety and welfare is my top priority."

Her scent enveloped him right before her arm pressed into his. Like a coward, he retreated and reversed course for the living room. Fortunately, most of the windows had blinds, which he shut. The wall-length windows weren't ideal, but at least they faced the rear of the property, and he would have a clear view if anyone tried to approach them from the beach.

He climbed the stairs to the second floor and performed a thorough search before returning to the main level where Fallon waited for him.

"I, uh, overheard your conversation with Ciaran this morning," she hedged.

He arched an eyebrow, assuming her former position by the expansive glass. "You mean you eavesdropped."

She shrugged. "Semantics," she said, flicking his accusation off with a wave of her fingers. "Anyway, he mentioned Tristan." She hesitated, and he almost turned away from the soft, but incisive, scrutiny. The suspicion of Tristan's duplicity tasted like acrid ashes in his mouth and nose, even as his heart fought against the possibility. "Do you really believe he's capable of betraying you?"

"No. Yes. Hell, I don't know," he murmured. Closing his eyes, he shifted so he no longer remained captive to the aching sympathy in her gaze. It tempted him to drag her close, bury his face in the fragrant haven between her neck and shoulder, and breathe her deep into his lungs. "I don't want to believe it. We grew up together; we were as close as brothers."

"Were?"

A pang echoed in his chest, and he rubbed a palm over it. "Things have been...different between us. Especially since Marcus died..." He shook his head. "Tristan distanced himself. Started pursuing his career with a vengeance that seemed to border on obsessive. For a while there, I was worried about him. But then Joy entered his life." An image of the tall, stunning blonde who loved his best friend and had brought the light back into his face and heart wavered in his head. "For the past two years, he's returned to being the man I knew. A part of me—the part that played kickball together, snuck our first beer together, cried over a friend's grave together—can't accept that Tristan could be the leak.

But I can't ignore the facts either."

A gentle hand settled on his lower back, and she leaned her head against his shoulder. They stood like that for several long moments, her silent support so needed, but as much as he wanted—craved to—he didn't grab onto it.

She lifted her head, tilted it back, and he stared down into her beautiful face. All those curls tumbled around her face and shoulders like contained sunshine. The beams from the late-morning sun captured in her skin. Jesus, he couldn't decide whether he wanted to bask in her heat or lick her smooth flesh and find out if it tasted like the sweet honey it resembled.

He couldn't do either.

"Shane," she whispered, cupping his jaw.

"You should go get unpacked while I finish checking the house out."

Again, that flash of hurt. But this time he ignored it. Walked away from it before he once more did something stupid they would both come to regret. Like surrender to the hunger coursing through his veins and pounding in his cock.

Coming here with her had been a bad idea. He'd been so smug, so damn arrogant he could resist her. That he could manhandle and control his reluctant attraction toward her. That her scent wasn't as delicious, the need to taste her not as demanding.

If there was a bigger fool alive on this earth, they both should be locked up for their own safety.

Chapter Eleven

Some people enjoyed the quiet. Found it soothing. Comforting.

Fallon had never been one of those people.

On bare feet, she descended the stairs from the second floor, escaping the stifling silence of her bedroom. As a child and even later as a teen, she'd often been accused of being too noisy or rambunctious. Which, okay, had been true. With a neglectful mother and workaholic father, she'd been alone most of the time except for the company of whatever nanny-of-the-month. The quiet had seemed to taunt her, driving home the fact that neither parent thought her special or lovable enough to spend time with. Silence was an indictment on her worthiness.

One she'd had a tough time disputing.

So she'd filled it with music, talking, television—anything.

Years later, old habits died hard.

Yet, the need to fill the vacuum of noise comprised only half the reason she was roaming through the house hours after arriving. Night had fallen, and she and Shane had shared a subdued dinner before Shane had holed himself up in the den, and she'd retired to her room for the evening. The voluntary seclusion had lasted thirty minutes.

From their first meeting when Shane had picked Addisyn up outside the local children's theater where she and Fallon had been taking lessons, she'd been drawn to him. Then she could chalk it up to a girl's crush on an older, gorgeous boy. As the years passed, the infatuation had deepened into more, and the pull never decreased in power but intensified. Even the disastrous kiss and their estrangement hadn't diminished the strength of the tug on her heart when Addisyn mentioned his name or the rare occasions they occupied the same space.

With his abrupt and dramatic reappearance in her life, the draw had converted into a need. A need to be near him, inhale his scent, study his reserved but insanely sexy features. And after this morning…

A shudder rippled through her. She would never forget the sudden explosion of glass, the deadly hum of bullets slicing through the air, his big frame crushing her to the floor, covering her, protecting her…the terror pumping through her veins, strangling her as he hid her in the hall closet before closing the door to face possible death. For her.

Before she'd been shut into darkness, she'd frantically drank in the forbidding lines of his face, the harsh slash of his mouth, the rage darkening his turquoise eyes to that of a roiling, turbulent sea…prayed that same face would greet her when the door opened again.

She'd come so close to losing him. And whether he was avoiding or ignoring her, she'd didn't care. As long as he still lived and breathed in all his anal glory. She couldn't imagine a world without him in it.

"Oh shit!"

The bellow thundered from the back of the house in the direction of the kitchen. She froze on the bottom step. *Shane.* That roar had come from Shane. *Oh God, Michaels found us.* Fear gripped her, snatching control of her muscles and rendering her motionless. Except for her heart that raced like a runaway horse in her chest. Panic had colored his voice. Reserved, taciturn Shane who remained cool in the face of flying bullets sounded...scared.

It was this thought that melted her deep freeze.

She shot off the step and darted down the hall. Breath harsh in her ears, she skidded to a halt in the kitchen entrance. Shane stood in front of the counter, a living statute with his arms outstretched, his gun clasped in his hands. She scanned the room, searching for the threat that had caused the alarm in his tone and forced him to draw his weapon. Inspecting the entrance that led into the dining room, the corners, and the large, dark picture window, she frowned. Nothing. The room was empty.

Confused, she returned her attention to Shane.

"Shane?"

He didn't turn to look at her, but shifted back a couple of steps, the movement careful, cautious as if he edged around a land mine.

"Shane?" she repeated, softer this time, worry worming its way through her veins. "What? What's wrong?"

He cocked his head to the side, but his gaze and gun remained focused on whatever it was she couldn't see.

"Spider," he ground out.

Her frown deepened, confusion supplanting the concern. "Um…huh?"

"Spider," he repeated. "There's a spider."

O-kay. She moved farther into the room until she stood next to him, still sweeping the area, certain she'd find an outside threat. But as her gaze passed over the wall in back of the kitchen table and chairs, she did spot a dark brown spider huddled against the white baseboard.

"Yeah, it is," she agreed, tilting her head. About an inch and a half in size, thick, and hairy, the thing was butt ugly but… She shrugged. "Looks like a wolf spider."

"I don't give a damn if it's a freaking elephant spider," he growled. "We can't occupy the same space." He shot her a glance. "Do spiders bother you?"

She shook her head. "No. Now if a snake came out of that cabinet, I'd blow this place up. But, nah, I'm good with spiders."

He nodded. "Good. Get rid of it." A muscle in his jaw flexed. "Or I can just put a bullet in it."

"For the love of…" She rolled her eyes. "Put the gun down, Rambo." She placed a hand on the barrel and lowered the weapon and his arms. "I'll just take it outside—"

"And have it find its way back in?" He shook his head. "Hell no. Kill it."

"Shane…"

"Kill. It." A pause. "Please."

One look at his cold features and stiff frame, and the objection died on her lips. Well damn, he was really afraid of it. "Okay, fine. I got it."

Turning around, she grabbed the broom and dustpan from the corner. In a matter of minutes the spider was smashed and halfway to the garbage can.

"Wait," Shane barked. "What are you doing?"

She jerked to a stop. "Uh, throwing it out."

"You can't put it in the trash. Flush it down the toilet."

She nodded slowly. Blinked. Blinked again. "Riiight. Because it can resurrect if it's in there as opposed to the toilet."

His eyes narrowed on her, his mouth a grim line. "It happened to a man once; I'm not taking any chances."

Snorting, she strode past him—and swallowed a snicker as he eased back a step when she passed with the dead insect. Minutes later, after sending the arachnid off for a burial at sea, she returned to the kitchen.

"Funny," she drawled, hopping up on the marble island, "I don't remember you being afraid of spiders when we were younger."

"You're finding a little too much joy in this," he said, tucking his weapon in his shoulder holster.

"Oh no." She widened her eyes. "Of course not. There's nothing to be ashamed of. Nope." Her mouth twitched, and she struggled to control the uncontrollable quirk.

"Uh-huh." He arched an eyebrow. "To answer your question, I wasn't afraid of them before I entered the Army. But over in Afghanistan they have these abominations called camel spiders. Big as fuck with fangs and the fuckers can run up to ten miles per hour. First time I saw one I almost went AWOL. Now I can't stand any of 'em. Small, big, I don't care. I hate them. Last week I saw one in the office bathroom, and Ciaran had to kill the thing for me. He hasn't let me hear the end of it yet."

At the picture of Ciaran running to Shane's rescue in the men's restroom, she lost the battle of holding in the laughter she'd been fighting since killing the wolf spider. Throwing her head back, she hooted, the evil glee of this big alpha male shrinking in the face of a little insect rolling up in her and spilling out in huge, gut-aching belly laughter. She sucked in several breaths, glanced at his wry expression, and dissolved into a bout of hilarity once more.

"I'm so glad I could amuse you," he snapped.

"I-I'm sorry." She gasped. "Seriously..."

"Oh yeah," he drawled. "I got that out of the gasps for breath." Grunting, he moved to the coffeemaker and hit the power button.

"My bad, Shane," she wheezed. Inhaling, she wiped the moisture from under her eyes. "Tell you what," she added, jumping down off the island. "I'll make the coffee to make it up to you."

"I got it." He reached for the cabinet handle above him.

"And if there are more spiders hanging out inside there...?"

His fingers flexed around the knob before he slowly lowered his arm.

"Yeah." He cleared his throat. "Cups are up there. Thanks. I have some calls to make."

"No problem," she said, grinning.

Before long, she had his coffee—black with one spoonful of sugar—in one hand and a cup for herself in the other. Carefully balancing the hot brews, she headed toward the den.

"...already talked to Rafe. He should be sending you a report on Tristan's finances in the next few hours."

Tristan? She frowned, drawing to a halt outside the entrance. A peek around the jamb revealed Shane perched on the dark brown leather couch, his cell phone pressed to his ear. Easing back, his previous accusation of eavesdropping fresh in her mind, she settled in to listen.

"If he's been on the take, this case wouldn't be the first. I have Rafe searching for any deposits or purchases inconsistent with an officer's salary in the last three years." Pause and a weary sigh. "Yeah, this will help in either clearing Tristan…or condemning him." Another pause, this one longer. "Rafe agreed to get right on it. After he contacts you, call me immediately, okay?"

He bid the person on the other end good-bye, and silence permeated the room.

"You can stop lurking in the hall and come in now," he called out, his voice as dry as an African desert in the height of a summer drought. Pretty damn dry.

She grimaced. *Busted*. Smoothing out her expression, she pasted on a smile and sauntered into the room.

"Hey," she greeted brightly, setting the coffee cups on the table before dropping onto the love seat across from him. Shane arched a dark brow in response. "Okay, fine. You caught me." She shrugged. "Who's Rafe?"

After a long moment, he shook his head, the barest hint of a smile quirking a corner of his sensual mouth. "He's a friend and co-owner of Liberty Security Services, a firm we sometimes do contract work for. He's also a computer genius."

"Who's pulling Tristan's financial records? Isn't that, oh I don't know, illegal?"

"Only if he gets caught. And Raphael Marcel is too good to get caught," he said, his admiration for the other man clear. "Besides, these days Rafe only uses his powers for good. He, more than anyone, understands protecting those you love at whatever cost. It's why he's made an exception for us."

"Have you ever done something 'at whatever cost'?" she asked, tucking her feet beneath her on the sofa.

He stared at her, and all traces of amusement disappeared behind an aloof mask. "I was in a war, Fallon," he said, voice devoid of all emotion.

She hated the emptiness…no, the desolation captured in those five words. In that awful closed expression. Intuition hinted he most likely never spoke of his time in Afghanistan. Or the shooting and injury that had brought him back home.

"The other night I noticed you wear three dog tags." She touched her chest, and continued in spite of the forbidding hardness entering his eyes. "I thought most soldiers had two."

Silence so cold entered the room, she wouldn't have been surprised if icicles formed in front of her nose. Damn, she should've left it alone. Shouldn't have pushed…

"One of them is Marcus's," he said in that same flat tone. "I have one, and Khalil has the other."

"Khalil," she murmured. "I know he's a partner in GDG, but I've never met him."

"He served with Marcus and me in Afghanistan."

A deep silence followed his admission, and she could fill in the blanks from what little Addy had managed to pry from Shane about the attack that had injured him and several of his fellow soldiers. The attack that had ended his military career. The attack where Marcus had sacrificed his life to save his friends.

"Shane, I didn't—"

"It's fine." Translation: *Mind your business. I don't want to talk about it.*

Tension invaded the room, an intruder she had no idea how to cast out. Especially when she'd opened the door and invited it in.

Desperate to see a smile on his face for once—or even the exasperation reserved just for her—she leaned forward, resting her elbows on her knees.

"Truth or dare," she blurted.

Surprise flared in his eyes, the only reaction to her impulsive announcement. "What?"

"Truth or dare," she repeated, warming up to the idea. "Let's play." When he studied her as if she'd suggested running down to the beach bare-ass naked and jumping in the ocean, she sighed. "Come on. What else do we have to do?"

"Oh, I'm sure I can think of something else," he drawled, rising from the couch.

"Y'know, a while back I asked Addy if you'd had that two-by-four removed from your ass." She cocked her head to the side, pretending to peer at the back of his black cargo pants. "I see it's still firmly embedded."

His eyes narrowed. "I swear that mouth. Never. Stops." But he sank down, reclaiming his seat on the sofa. "Fine," he agreed. "Let's play."

Overlooking his lack of enthusiasm, she grinned. Stick up his ass or not, he was such a man. Insult their pride or their dick, and they crumbled. "Truth or dare?"

Crossing his arms, he bit out, "Truth."

"*Ba-KAH,*" she squawked, her chicken imitation earning a hard glare. "Okay, okay." She laughed, holding her hands up in the age-old sign of surrender. Tapping a finger against her bottom lip, she scrunched her face as if deep in thought. *Not.* She propped her chin in her palms. "What is your favorite sexual position?"

"What the hell kind of question is that?" he snapped, fire flashing in his gaze. But not anger. She'd glimpsed his anger—the emotion turned his eyes into icy shards. But desire, lust…it smoldered so he stared at her with heat that singed her senses, lit a clenching deep in her sex. Nope, he wasn't angry.

"One that requires a truthful answer," she purred.

"My favorite sexual position." He leaned forward, bracing his forearms on his thighs. His piercing scrutiny ensnared her, didn't allow her to move, to breathe. "A woman under me, her thighs spread wide, riding my waist, taking me deep. From this position I can control how hard or gentle, fast or slow I fuck. I can study what makes her tremble, gasp, or cry out. Come." His hooded stare roamed her face, landed on her parted lips where low pants escaped. "Truth or dare?" he murmured.

Truth or what…? Oh God, *right.* "Dare."

An evil smile eased across his face, and her belly dipped. "You have to…be quiet for five minutes."

Her jaw dropped. Actually. Dropped. "Are you freakin' kidding me?"

"That's the dare. Unless you refuse…" He lifted a broad shoulder. "I think there are consequences for that."

"Fine," she ground out, scowling as he set the stopwatch on his cell phone.

For the following five minutes she fought against the urge to talk. Thoughts popped into her head, and more than once she almost blurted them out. So she settled for glaring holes into Shane's chest. And consigning his balls to the most violent shade of blue possible.

"Time," he announced when the alarm on the cell beeped. "I do believe that's the longest I've ever heard you quiet. Well, except when you're asleep."

"Truth. Or. Dare," she growled.

"Dare."

Oh, payback was a bitch. "Sing 'Danny Boy.'" She hooted at his stunned, blank expression. "Oh yeah," she crowed. "Unless you refuse…" she repeated his earlier veiled threat, mimicking his shrug as well. "Then we would have to move onto the double-dog dare area."

"How old are we?" he grumbled under his breath, shooting her a fierce scowl.

"Listen, you can concede. I can't promise everyone won't know how you quit 'cause you were scared—"

The first notes of "Danny Boy" boomed into the air.

And she discovered that Shane Roarke possessed at least one imperfection: his singing voice.

She winced, still managing to maintain a straight face as he bade Danny Boy to come back when summer was upon the meadow, the high note a mangled cross between two cats shadowboxing and a dying buffalo. But by the time he sang of sweet dreams and sleeping in peace, she'd lost it. Clutching her aching stomach, she flopped on the couch cushions, hollering in laughter. Tears leaked from her eyes as she gasped for breath.

Good God, he was awful. Like eternal-punishment-in-the-bowels-of-Tartarus awful. And it was wonderful. Sitting up, she wiped the moisture from her cheeks, pressing her hands to her sore abdomen. Jesus, when was the last time she'd laughed so hard? Months. Even before she witnessed the murder. It was cathartic. Freeing.

And Shane had gifted it to her.

He studied her, a slight smile tipping a corner of his full mouth. "Truth or dare," he murmured.

"Truth."

The other corner quirked. "Now who's chicken?" he softly taunted.

"Chicken," she said raising one hand, palm up. "Self-preservation," she added, lifting the other hand. Shrugging, she "weighed" her options. Self-preservation won. "I can live with chicken."

"Speaking of chicken." He cocked his head to the side. "What are you most afraid of?"

She blinked, momentarily surprised. "Afraid of?"

"Yes," he said, leaning forward. "As long as I've known you, fear has never been in your vocabulary. Indomitable, willful, bold. But everyone's scared of something. What about you?"

She chuckled, the sound strained, forced. "Besides birthdays? Because they terrify the bejeezus out of me. Especially since on my last one I witnessed a murder."

But the joke fell flat under his unblinking contemplation, and her tongue lay in her mouth like a block of cement. His words reverberated in her head, and suddenly her cowardice at deflecting his question shamed her.

Was that how he really perceived her? Fearless. When she was terrified of every damn thing? Part of her—the vain part—loathed to change his perception. She wanted to be seen as strong and brave by this man whose profession had been battle and defense, and who still provided security and safety. But the game was Truth or Dare. And the other half of her, the half that yearned to share a piece with him that she hadn't revealed to anyone else, longed to give him her truth.

"Failing," she admitted softly, shifting her eyes to his chest. "I'm afraid of failing at being more than a spoiled socialite who lives off her parents, only to one day marry and sponge off her husband. I'm afraid of failing at succeeding. I'm afraid of failing at living, at *becoming*." Her chest rose and fell on rapid breaths. The truth, it seemed, was also terrifying. Especially when the person on the receiving end had the power to crush your heart and spirit with it. Gathering her pride and courage, she met his gaze again. And encountered an understanding and heat that stole her the air from her lungs. "And birthdays," she added, reaching for flippant and falling flat.

His eyebrow winged high. "What?"

"Birthdays," she repeated. "I'm afraid of them, too." She inhaled, released it on a humorless chuckle. "I bet I could go into the *Guinness Book of World Records* for the suckiest birthdays on record. I've sat on a window seat and waited hours for my father to pick me up, only to have him be a no show. I threw myself at you and lost my virginity to a pompous, inept ass on the same birthday." She snickered. "On the last one, my boyfriend broke up with me by Twitter, and I witnessed a murder. You tell me, where do I go from there?"

"Twitter?" he croaked, zeroing in on that particular humiliating detail. "You're fucking kidding me."

"Asshole didn't even have the decency to direct message me. He tweeted it to God and country."

"And you did…what?"

She shrugged, attempting nonchalance. "Tweeted back he shouldn't worry about his small dick or little performance problem." She paused. "And included a picture of his junk."

"Oh. Shit." He stared at her, blinked several times, then threw his head back and hooted, shaking with his hilarity. "You emasculated a man with social media."

"In one hundred and forty characters. I rock."

"Yeah, you do." He laughed, but eventually quieted, studying her with knowing eyes. "I know a little something about screwed up birthdays, too."

She straightened, stunned. A rueful half smile quirked the corner of his mouth

"I...hated my birthday. Not because no one would re-member or give a damn. I dreaded my birthday because my mother *would* remember. She never forgot one. Not for me or Addy." His lips straightened into a sober line. "My stom-ach would hollow out every time Addy's or mine neared. Mom would rent hotel ballrooms to throw huge, outrageous parties complete with DJs, catering, clowns and magicians when we were younger. She went all out...and afterward our money was all out. Nothing for rent, groceries, or utili-ties. I've lost count of how many parties were followed by days in the dark eating peanut butter and jelly sandwiches, waiting for the letter on the door about late rent — or worse, an eviction notice because the previous month's rent had gone unpaid, too."

The urge to touch him, cradle his cheek, and kiss away the hurt and anger he probably wasn't even aware tainted his voice, swirled inside her. She would bet money he'd never confided in anyone about those days. Not to his friends, and definitely not Addisyn, to whom he'd had to be the strong, protective big brother. Strange how they could find something as obscure—and bruising—as birthday tragedies in common.

"Truth or dare," he murmured.

"Wait." She held up a hand. "Hold on. It's my turn."

"I just admitted a truth. So," he shook his head, "my turn again."

She scowled. "No fair. I didn't agree to that."

He chuckled, and the low, wicked rumble of amusement stroked over her skin, slipped beneath her T-shirt to caress her nipples into hard tips before snaking under her jeans to circle her clit. Leaving her hot, flushed, and aching. His gaze dropped to her breasts, and no way in hell he could miss the rigid points poking against the thin cotton. Her breath snagged in her lungs, and remained there until his scrutiny rose to her face again. The heat there singed her, tossed kindling on the fire already simmering in her veins.

"Life rarely is fair, baby," he said, the endearment another caress to her already sensitized senses. "Now. Truth or dare."

"Fine," she bit out. "Truth."

"Truth," he repeated, his hooded scrutiny piercing, glittering. "Last night you asked what if all you wanted from me was to fuck? No strings, just sex. Was that true? Do you just want to be…taken?"

She should lie. Self-preservation—the same defense mechanism that had been off the clock when she'd kissed him all those years ago—shouted to deflect, pass the outburst off as an impetuous taunt. To save herself from further humiliation. But the same need and dangerous lick of anticipation curled in her chest, her belly, compelling her to leap.

And damn the fall.

"I know why you believe getting involved with me would be the height of lunacy. Addy, I'm her best friend. It could get messy. Not to mention that you think I'm reckless, irresponsible. I'm aware of what you want for your life. The family, wife, the American dream. I even understand why. But what you don't understand is that's not *my* dream. You want to know what is my dream?" she whispered. "To be that woman under you. To be spread wide and covered. To be held down, touched, filled until I can't take anymore. And then have you prove me wrong." She curled her fingers into the couch beside her thighs, her heart thumping behind her sternum like a rabbit late for tea. "I don't want forever. I never did... I just want right now."

Except for the small tic jumping along his tightly clenched jaw, he didn't move. Not one muscle. But those eyes... How could she have ever thought of them as cold, aloof? Molten. And with a searing intensity that spoke of the previous night when she'd crawled on the bed and took him into her mouth.

"Truth or dare," she whispered.

If possible, the inner fire in his gaze blazed brighter. "Truth," he uttered, that silk and gravel voice eliciting a shiver over her skin.

"If you could kiss me anywhere on my body right now, where would it be?"

He didn't reply, and for a devastating moment, her heart seized. She'd pushed too far, too fast. *Stupid*. He hadn't pushed her away from him in the shadowed cocoon of sensuality and darkness, but in the harsh light of this room, face-to-face, and clearheaded, his cool logic would prevail.

Leaving her standing out there on that ledge by herself... again.

"Forget—" She held a hand up as if she could stop the eminent rejection.

One moment he imitated a statue on the couch, and in the next he loomed over her, forcing her to lean back. His palms pressed the cushions on either side of her shoulders, caging her between the sofa and his big body. She regarded him, stunned into silence. His wide frame blocked out the room, so all that existed for her was him. His burning gaze, the carnal curves of his lips, the lust stamped on his hard, gorgeous features. The broad expanse of his shoulders and chest, the corded strength of his thighs as he herded closer.

"Your mouth," he purred like a powerful, rumbling predator, slipping free of his holster and setting it on the cushion. "You sucked me to heaven last night. Seeing your lips wrapped around my cock"—his eyes briefly closed before opening and snagging her again—"prettiest sight I've ever seen. I had to fight not to come the second you took me in." He brushed a thumb over her bottom lip. Pressed it so her teeth lightly abraded the tender skin on the inside. "But you've had my dick in your mouth, and I haven't even kissed you. That's a tragedy. A crime. You deserve more honor than that."

Removing his hand, he lowered his head so their noses bumped, and she could taste the flavor of his kiss on his breath.

"Open wide," he gently, but firmly, ordered. "Like you did for my cock. I want all of you."

I want all of you. Though the demand referred to her body, it still resonated deep within her where the neglected child and discarded—expendable—woman hid. The words incited a tremor that she had to consciously, ruthlessly quell. Lust. It glittered in his eyes. That's what this kiss entailed, not a claiming. Not that she desired it anyway. She belonged to herself—the only person who wouldn't hurt her, ignore her, throw her away.

In spite of the thoughts swirling in her head, she obeyed him. Nebulous longings and confusion rode the backseat to desire. She *craved* his kiss. Had fantasized about it for years. Not just the kiss, but the hunger that now brightened his gaze. The strain and tension fairly vibrating off him, evidence of his barely restrained control.

Unfolding her legs, she settled her feet on the floor, her thighs spread wide in invitation for him to move closer. She rested her hands on her lap, palms up in total submission to him, and tilted her head back.

With a low, almost animalistic growl, he swooped in, captured her lips, branded her with the hard thrust of his tongue. He swept inside, licking, stroking, devouring. Thrusting a hand in her hair, he tugged on the curls, while his other hand cupped and squeezed her jaw, commanding without words that she open wider, surrender more. With a moan, she did.

And he proceeded to fuck her mouth.

Raw and painfully erotic, nothing else could describe how he took her. Lips locked over hers, he plunged his tongue in and out, back and forth, consuming her. It wasn't gentle but carnal, wild. He rode her mouth as hard as she imagined him riding her. Not content to remain a passenger, she curled her tongue around his and sucked, drew on him. Above her, he shuddered.

His harsh, almost angry-sounding groan was her only warning before her world flipped upside down. She blinked, momentarily disoriented as the ceiling filled her vision instead of Shane. A hard surface pressed against her spine and lower back. The coffee table. She lay on the coffee table like high tea. And as strong, determined fingers worked at her jeans and cool air kissed her stomach and hips, she shivered with the sneaking suspicion she was about to become a meal.

"Oh God." Her breath snagged in her throat as Shane wrenched the tight denim down her legs and tossed them to the side, her panties quickly following suit. She stretched out before him naked from the waist down, vulnerable, exposed, and so turned on, he could surely see the evidence of it on the swollen folds of her sex.

Large, firm hands pushed her thighs apart, his thumbs caressing the seams that connected torso to legs. The air in the room thickened to the consistency of maple syrup, smothering her, filling her lungs. She flung an arm over her eyes, the other hand clutching the edge of the table. Holding on.

A part of her acknowledged she should possess at least some amount of modesty or reserve. Maybe put up a token resistance at his sudden and unsolicited baring or murmur an objection. She should… But her shouting anything other than "*Please, eat me!*" would be hypocritical. She wanted this—*craved* this.

"Shane," she whispered, begging, so damn ready.

Yet she wasn't ready.

Not for the swipe of his tongue parting her feminine lips. Not for the lazy swirl and greedy suckle to her clit. Not for the long, blunt finger thrusting inside her. She cried out, her back bowing off the table. Abandoning her grip, she reached for him, her fingertips glancing his dark strands. But when he dipped his head, licking the entrance his fingers stroked in and out of, he eluded her. She extended her arms over her head, grasping the edge once more.

"God, you're tight. So wet and tight," he praised, working another digit inside her, stretching her, causing a delicious burn to simmer in her pussy. And when he latched onto her clit again, the burn burst into a conflagration. The torturous suction and tug to the bundle of nerves and the steady pump of his fingers in her core, propelled her closer and closer to the edge. She couldn't control her hips, the frantic writhing and grinding of her sex against his voracious, erotic kiss. She didn't try to control it. The pleasure, so intense it skated the rim of sweet agony, swelled up and over her in relentless undulations again and again.

"That's it, baby," he murmured against her flesh, the closed fingers of his fist bumping against her folds as he finger-fucked her. "Let go. Come for me."

As if the permission was all her quivering body needed, she stiffened, a sharp, keening scream escaping her throat and bouncing off the walls. Ecstasy sucked her down into a dark vortex, and shaking, shuddering, she willingly dove into the deep.

Chapter Twelve

Shane's sneakered feet pounded against the sand. Sweat coated his brow, temples, and chest as he ran along the beach, his white T-shirt clinging to him in patches. A breeze blew in off the ocean, cooling his overheated skin. Too bad it didn't do a thing for his thoughts or the relentless ache in his balls.

Slowing his punishing pace, he propped his fists on his hips and studied the seemingly endless stretch of sand. As if its many grains contained the answers to the questions whirling around his head like a leaf caught up in a spring rainstorm. Primary among them, *what was he doing?*

He shouldn't have tasted her mouth last night. Shouldn't have laid her out on the coffee table and gorged himself on the sweetest pussy he'd ever savored. Their first kiss seven year ago he could blow off as a "Fallon thing"—impulsive, harmless. But during that damn game of Truth or Dare, he'd been the instigator. He'd crossed the room and tangled his fingers in her hair. He'd commanded her to open up for him.

He'd peeled her jeans away and ate her like a starving man seated at a 99-cent all-you-can-eat buffet.

And still walked away starving.

"Jesus," he muttered, turning to stare at the vast expanse of ocean. He squinted against the faint glare courtesy of the morning sun on the water. When hitting the beach, his intention had been seeking peace and a settling of his mind on this quiet, isolated stretch of shore. Whether through the brutal pace he'd set for himself or the serenity of the view, he'd hoped solutions would come to him.

But here he stood, sweaty, tired, and just as confused as when he'd jogged down the beach steps.

For years he'd managed to keep his distance from Fallon. His attraction was never an issue. *Attraction*. He snorted. Such an inadequate, anemic word to describe the gut-wrenching greed that snatched him up in its teeth like a chew toy whenever they shared the same space. The intensity of this, this *thing* between him and Fallon had been a powerful incentive in remembering why he couldn't touch her. Something that strong would be addictive, not satisfied by one night of sweating up the sheets and losing himself in her. She could make him forget why they were so wrong for each other. Make him long for more...

But Fallon didn't want more.

He scrubbed his palms over his head before dragging them down his face. Stubble from the jaw he hadn't paused to shave abraded his hands.

With one admission, she'd shattered the cuffs chaining his hands — and his will.

God only knew how long they would be forced to live under the same roof. But the day would eventually come when Jonah Michaels was caught, and she would testify against him. And when that day did arrive, their time cut off from the rest of the world would end.

Until then, why couldn't he indulge in the ecstasy he'd tasted last night?

Heat pumped through his blood and twisted his gut before throbbing in his cock like a second heartbeat. But none of it compared to the thud of his heart against his sternum as the seed of thought took root in his mind.

For however long they had locked away here, he could have her as much as he wanted, any way he wanted. Every fantasy that ever caused him to wake up with his hand wrapped around his erection could be realized. Pivoting, he studied the house at the top of the hill. The house where Fallon waited. The house that could become his heaven or hell. Or both.

No strings attached, she'd claimed.

Just sex.

It would be their secret. They could take their pleasure with no guilt, no commitment, no hearts involved. And when they left the safe house, they would return to their regular lives. The perfect arrangement. At least it would be if she agreed to it.

Clenching his jaw, he started jogging toward the beach stairs. She had to agree. Because after last night, no way he could keep his hands off her. Or his dick from inside her.

As he cleared the top of the steps, his cell vibrated against his hip. That could be Ciaran with the information about Tristan's financials. Or Rafe himself calling. He removed the phone from the pocket of his running shorts and glanced down at the screen. His jaw clenched, anger liberally doused with grief and guilt, curled in his chest.

Tristan.

His fingers tightened around the phone. A part of himself writhed with guilt over suspecting and investigating his friend—his best friend. The boy who'd fearlessly faced down any bully and later became the man who protected the city of Boston from deadlier bullies shouldn't be capable of the cold-blooded actions of the last couple of days. Wasn't capable, his heart argued. But his mind warned him that sentiment could blind him. Worse. Possibly get Fallon killed.

Locking his emotions behind an icy vault door, he swiped his thumb across the answer bar and pressed the phone to his ear.

"Are you okay?" Tristan barked. No "hello" or "Where are you?" but concern.

"Yes," Shane replied. "Both Fallon and I are fine."

"Thank God." Relief colored Tristan's voice. "I called Ciaran, but he didn't give me much information." A beat of silence passed over the line. "What the hell happened, Shane? When I got the call about shots fired at your address, I almost lost it. And then by the time I arrived you'd disappeared. No sign of you or Fallon. Why did you leave the scene?"

"Because the three assholes who'd just shot up my house to hell and back had escaped. I didn't know how long it would be before they, or some of their boys, would return to finish the job. And I chose not to wait around and find out."

"Where are you? I need to get statements from both you and Fallon. Ciaran said you were at a safe house. I can come to you—"

"No."

"Damn it, Shane," Tristan snarled. "This is the third attempt on her life in as many days. A bomb on a public street and then an assault in the clear of day. That house looks like a war zone. No one has been hurt—yet. But with the utter disregard they've shown, it's only a matter of time. Now I need a statement, need you two to come in and look at pictures to try and identify the perps at your place. I need *something*. The media has the city in an uproar over this. I can't protect you from this end if you don't help me."

Propping a fist on his hip, Shane tilted his head back to stare at the rear of the beach house. Where Fallon was tucked inside. Safe. *No way*. He shook his head. *No way in hell.*

"I'm not bringing Fallon to meet you. But," he continued, raising his voice above Tristan's immediate objection, "I'll come to Boston. Fallon didn't see anything that could help you, anyway. I saw the faces of the bastards the night at her apartment and yesterday morning. So tomorrow. Eleven o'clock." Providing statements and perusing mug shots would only bolster the case against Jonah Michaels and the Lords of War. But more than that, he needed to stare into Tristan's eyes and discern for himself if his friend was betraying him.

A thunderous quiet vibrated down the connection, reverberating in his ear.

"Where?" Tristan finally asked. Fury pulsed in the word, the tone.

Quickly, Shane scanned through locations that would provide privacy, protection, and sufficient cover for the team he planned on having at the ready. A grin curved his mouth as the perfect idea bloomed in his head.

"The police department parking lot."

• • •

Midmorning sunshine streamed in the floor-to-ceiling living room windows, hitting the glossy pages of the magazine Fallon flipped through. A tall floral arrangement of calla lilies and long strings of teardrop crystals set in a fluted glass vase caught her eye. Instantly in love, she picked up the scissors from the low glass table she'd stationed herself at and cut the picture from the page. The image joined the other growing stack next to her elbow.

During Shane's tour of the residence the day before, she'd noticed several home decorating periodicals in the guestrooms and en suite bathrooms. After a sleepless night, she'd waited until she'd heard Shane leave the house for a run before climbing out of bed, showering, and gathering up the magazines. From the school of asking forgiveness rather than permission, she'd scooped them up, carried them to the living room, and settled on the floor to peruse the pages for ideas.

When the trial finally commenced and she testified and reclaimed her life, everything in the stack of clippings—the flowers, bows, tomato bruschetta hors d'oeuvres, glazed salmon—would be hers. If the past month, especially the last couple of days, had taught her anything, it was time—and life—had no guarantees attached. And the event-planning company she'd dreamed about, had slaved under an ungrateful barracuda for, would no longer be a nebulous "one day." She would have it. Sooner rather than later.

She turned another page and studied the photo of a smiling groom dipping his laughing bride over his arm. The male model, with his closely cropped black hair, strong jaw, and tall frame, reminded her of Shane. Well, except for the smile. If Shane had ever worn such a carefree, relaxed, joyful grin, she hadn't glimpsed it. Even when they'd been younger, he'd been mature for his age—too mature.

Trudy, God love her, was one of the warmest and friendliest women Fallon had ever met, but as a provider, protector, comforter, and disciplinarian? Not so much. Those titles had fallen on Shane's wide, but too young, shoulders. He'd picked Addy up from the acting classes he'd paid for by working two jobs even while attending school. He ensured his little sister completed her homework, was fed when Trudy's friends had consumed all the food in the house, and had a roof over her head when their mother spent her paychecks on something other than rent. While Trudy had been more loving and affectionate than Fallon's parents, their neglect was just opposite sides of the same coin.

She frowned down at the glossy magazine page. That protectiveness, it defined Shane. All his life he'd overcompensated for Trudy's lax parenting style with Addy. And it probably contributed to his refusal to become involved with Fallon. He wouldn't risk ruining his sister's friendship with Fallon—wouldn't hurt Addy by jeopardizing the relationship with the person she considered family. No, Shane wouldn't take the chance. Not even for a fling that would inevitably fall apart.

Maybe it'd been his steadfastness, stability, and strength that had initially drawn Fallon to him. He'd represented everything that had been missing in her life. But as she'd grown, the admiration had darkened and deepened to something hungrier, needier. Something that had less to do with his dependability and more to do with the masculine beauty of his turquoise eyes, Celtic marauder cheekbones, and sexy, full lips. And those lips. *Whoa, boy*.

She exhaled a shuddering breath. If she closed her eyes, she could feel the wicked press and suction of his diabolical mouth on her sex. Her core clenched and quivered as if anticipating the thrust of his fingers again. Or his cock. Jesus Christ, if his tongue and hand could blow her away like they did, actually having him inside her would probably send her into an ecstasy-induced coma. Or at least it would if he ever touched her again. Which, from the silent way he'd redressed her and then helped her from the floor before disappearing up the stairs, might be never. She heaved a sigh and sliced a path around a beautiful bouquet of jeweled brooches. With Shane, for every step they took forward, he ran a 5k backward.

"What are you doing?"

The rumble of his voice rolled down her spine and tripped over her skin before swan-diving between her legs. Turned on by *his freaking voice, for God's sake. Pathetic, thy name is Fallon.*

"Hey," she said, pumping a mental fist when her voice remained steady and nonchalant. "I didn't hear you come in from your run." *Lie.* She'd not only heard the back door open on his return but his bedroom door shut. Then her mind had gone on a skip through the tulips as she imagined him standing under the showerhead, water pouring down over his gorgeous body, drops just glistening... *Focus, damn it!* "Have you heard back from Rafe yet?" She might've heard his cell ring in his room earlier as she passed his bedroom. And she *miiiight've* slowed her pace to catch a snippet of his conversation. Might.

"Yes," he said. "He should have a report for me by this evening."

Cautious joy for him leaped in her chest. "Well no news is good news, right?" She glanced over her shoulder. "That means he's having to really dig deep to see if Tristan is receiving payoffs. There's nothing obvious."

"Yes," he agreed, but something in his voice caused her to frown.

"What? For someone who just found out there's a good chance his friend isn't stabbing him in the back, you sound markedly lackluster."

"I am…hopeful. But money isn't the only currency," he murmured. "I'm meeting up with him tomorrow morning. He needs a statement from us, and I'm going to look through some photos."

Shock rocketed through her. Setting the scissors on the table, she twisted around, gaped at him. Fear, worry, anger — the emotions coalesced inside her like a supernova set to explode.

"What? What are you talking about? Why can't you email or call in a statement? You can't leave…" What if it was a trap? A way to lure Shane out so Jonah Michaels and his gang could kill him?

"Wait." He held up a hand. "I'm not leaving you alone. My business partner, Khalil, is going to drive up and cover me here while I'm in Boston."

"I don't give a damn about me," she snapped. "You, Shane. Jonah Michaels knows who you are, too. Exhibit A, the new air-conditioning job on your house. You suspect Tristan might be working for him, and yet you're going to see him? Why don't you just air a public service announcement informing Michaels where you are?"

"One, we don't know for certain Tristan is on the take. But I intend to find out tomorrow."

"How?" she sniped. "Jedi mind trick? Do you really expect him to admit it if it's true?" She scrutinized his carefully blank expression, then released a sharp bark of disbelieving laughter. "You do, don't you?"

He crossed his arms over his chest. "Give me some credit, Fallon. *Star Wars* references aside, I've known him since we were kids. I know his tells like no one else." He frowned, glanced away. "I *need* to see him." Then, as if shaking the thought off, he narrowed his eyes on the stack of magazines on the table. "What are you doing?"

For a second, she debated whether to go along with the subtle—*not*—topic shift. But peering at the determined, stern lines of his face, she conceded and refocused on her cutting. "I'm scouring magazines for ideas."

"Ideas?" He lowered to the couch, his long legs sprawled out in front of him. A scant wedge of space separated her arm from his knee. "For what?"

She risked a glance at him, over her shoulder, and answered because she spied genuine interest in his gaze instead of polite indifference. "For future weddings."

"Excuse me?" he asked, voice suddenly tight. *Huh. Interesting.*

"For the future fairy-tale weddings I'll get to plan for other people once I have my life back and my company up and running."

"Oh." A heartbeat of silence. "Addisyn told me you were working for an event planner before the murder. I didn't know you wanted a career in the field."

She shot him a sideways look from under her lashes. "Right. You thought it was another dead-end job while I 'found myself.'" She gave the scissors a vicious snap, decapitating a bridesmaid in the process.

"Actually, I was proud of you for supporting yourself and forging your own path."

Well…damn. Didn't that just suck all the righteous wind out of her sails? At this point she should say something polite and conciliatory like *Thank you* or *I really appreciate that*. But then the image of his expression before walking away from her last night popped into her mind. Aloof. Cold. And she remained stubbornly silent.

Aaww. He said he was proud. It was sweet.

Ah shaddup.

Yeah, she was arguing with herself. *Ticket for one to Cray-cray-ville, please.*

"What made you decide to go into this field? Especially…"

"Especially since I have firsthand knowledge that marriage rarely outlasts the time it takes the ice sculpture to melt? Why would I, of all people, want to go into a business surrounding weddings?" She shook her head and flipped another page, picking up the scissors again. "While I don't buy into the happily-ever-after-forever line, I do believe in happy for now. And isn't that what any of us have? This current moment, the 'now'? Why not celebrate it, and help others to do the same? Besides, it's not just weddings. It's anniversaries. Birthdays. Or it's-Thursday-we-should-celebrate parties. To me, there's no better job in the world than bringing people joy and laughter. Or in creating precious memories they'll look back on years later, smile and reminisce about," she continued, voice thickening. She cleared her throat. "In a way, it's kind of like immortality because I leave a stamp on their lives."

She didn't look up from the magazine, not when he slid to the floor beside her, and not when a hard thigh pressed against hers. Looking up would require courage she didn't have at the moment, a vulnerability she wasn't prepared to expose to him. Well, not any more than she already had.

A gentle caress swept across her cheekbone. Her ear. Jaw.

She shivered. Closed her eyes. The scissors clattered to the table. *No fair.* After last night, he had to know how susceptible she was to his touch. He fought dirty.

"You'll do a wonderful job," Shane murmured. "But I've always known once you discovered something to funnel all of that amazing passion into, you would excel at whatever you set your mind to. And you're brilliant and stubborn enough to make a go of it." Her breath caught in her throat, trapped by the tenderness in his voice as well as the words.

She loosed a short bark of laughter, uncomfortable and teetering with this warmer, more open Shane. This Shane who willingly reached for her, comforted her.

"Well don't congratulate me just yet. I have to survive a hit man first, testify at his trial, and then find some way to scrape up seed money to fund this dream."

Addled from sitting so close to him and inhaling his wind and skin scent, she stood and strode over to the fully stocked bar she'd scoped out the night before. She slapped bottles of vodka and Kahlua on the polished top. Thanks to her stint as a bartender in college, she could fix a mean White Russian. And damn did she need one.

He quirked an eyebrow but refrained from uttering the *Little early in the day for drinking, isn't it?* the gesture implied.

"Why don't you ask your father? I'm sure he would loan it to you."

"Uh, no." She splashed vodka into a tall glass. "When I told him I didn't need his money, I meant it. Besides, I'm not prepared to get all tangled up in the strings he would attach to the request. Or anything I came to him for."

Shane rose, and his long strides slowly ate up the distance between them. "Fallon, you're a talker." He grimaced, rubbed a hand over the nape of his neck. "*God*, are you a talker."

"Well, aren't you a flatterer?" she drawled, halting midpour.

He held up his palms. "Hear me out," he said, lowering his arms. "Everyone doesn't know how to communicate like you. Some of us aren't shaped to, and then some of us are too scared." He paused, an emotion she couldn't decipher ghosting across his face. *Which one are you?* She studied his face, hungry for the answer. "Your father…he loves you. I'm not making excuses for him, but—"

She snorted, capping the Kahlua. "Dr. Phil says whenever you put a 'but' after a statement, you're saying 'ignore everything I've just said because now I'm about to tell you what I really mean.'"

He rolled his eyes and grumbled something under his breath that sounded a lot like, "Screw Dr. Phil." Which was just blasphemous.

"Fine," he ground out. "Maybe I am making an excuse. Work consumes him. Your mother has her men and numerous marriages, and he has his work. Ever stop to consider that maybe the reason he places distances between you and him is out of fear? Fear of being hurt again? Fear of rejection. At the same time, he tries to keep you in his life with the one thing he values, and he damn sure knows your mother cherishes. Money." His tone dropped to a low, husky rumble. "He doesn't know how to talk to you. How to handle you."

"I'm not a child who needs to be 'handled,' Shane. You make me sound like a bomb about to detonate and take out everyone and thing within a hundred-mile radius."

He chuckled, but his laughter contained a serrated, rusty edge. "You're not so far off the mark. That fire, spirit, and utter lack of fear can be daunting. Damn that. Downright scary. Especially when it stares you in the face."

Her throat worked, but no words emerged. The last part—had he been referring to his father...or himself? Stunned, she rewound the last few years through her head like a movie reel. The coldness. The aloofness. The reserve. All this time, had his behavior been rooted in fear instead of disgust? As soon as the thought occurred, she dismissed it. Not G.I. Joe. Mr. Ultimate Soldier. This was the same man who'd fought a war on foreign soil. A man who'd returned home after being gravely wounded only to enter into business providing security, still protecting and guarding people. Imagining Shane Roarke afraid ranked right up there with unicorns and leprechauns. Or zombie apocalypses. It could happen in a realm far, far away, but not likely.

"I'll think about it," she lied, sampling her drink, eager to drop the subject before she did something stupid like beg him to touch her again.

He didn't reply, didn't call bullshit. Instead, he plucked the glass from her hand, turned it, and raised the drink to his mouth, lips closing over the exact spot from which she'd sipped. Flames ignited in her belly, simmering like hot coals. *God, that was sexy*. Like they'd kissed without touching lips.

"Why were you fired from the event-planning job you had? I would think witnessing a murder would be a good excuse for missing a day."

A sour taste flooded her tongue, erasing the sweet flavor of the mixed alcohol. "I couldn't explain to my employer that the reason I didn't go to work that day was because I witnessed a murder. My identity was supposed to be kept under wraps, and that barracuda would've sold my name to the highest bidder. So when I didn't call in, she jumped on the chance to fire me. She'd been looking for a reason anyway. One that wouldn't draw a sexual-harassment lawsuit anyway." His eyebrows winged above his turquoise eyes, and she winced. God, what had been in that bottle? One sip and her lips were flapping like laundry hung on a clothesline. "Her troll son couldn't keep his hands off my ass even though I repeatedly warned him to keep his grubby little paws to himself. The last time he did it, I just happened to have a pair of scissors…"

"You stabbed him with scissors?"

"Poked." She shot up an admonishing finger. "Poked, not stabbed. Even though the cry baby whined like I took a butcher knife to him," she grumbled.

"Good."

Her head jerked up, and she gaped at him, incredulous. "Good?" she repeated.

"Yeah." He nodded, his full mouth firmed into a grim line. "He's lucky I wasn't there. I would've broken the grabby bastard's hand."

She slapped her palms on the bar top, leaned forward. "Okay, please help me to understand why my stabbing the boss's son was okay in your holy bible of decorum, but when I stink-bombed Dennis's car, you ripped me a new one?"

"The asshole touched you." He mimicked her pose, bending forward until their noses almost bumped. "On the other hand, you could've gone to jail for that stunt you pulled with Addy's ex. Criminal mischief. Vandalism. Burglary. But you didn't think about the consequences of your actions then, did you? You just didn't *think*."

"I did, too, think about it. I didn't care. He cheated on Addy—he hurt her. I was the one who held her while she cried. A night in jail and a fine would've been worth funking up his car. If you're expecting regret or an 'I'm sorry,' I hate to disappoint you *again*, but the devil will wear a fur coat and long johns before you hear those words from me."

"You just don't give a fuck, do you?"

She bared her teeth in a nasty grin. "Nope," she said, her lips popping on the "p."

Chapter Thirteen

A silence charged with tension and something darker—fiercer—snapped between them like a live, electrified wire. Shane's short, hard bursts of breath bathed Fallon's lips. His bright stare blazed, scorching her. Damn, he was pissed—

His arm snaked out. His hand snagged the back of her neck. Hauled her forward. His mouth crashed over hers. Took. Conquered. Consumed.

Just like last night.

And just like last night, she opened to him with a soft whimper, surrendered. His tongue penetrated her lips, thrust in a perfect imitation of another, deeper claiming. She moaned, and he tugged her around the bar, never once breaking contact. Teeth clacked, tongues tangled. His taste…*good God* his taste. The flavor of him exploded in her mouth, so strong and potent her head swam. He, the kiss, his taste—it was fierce, raw, explicit. And she loved it.

She balled her fists into his sweater. Clung to him.

Demanding fingers burrowed in her hair, gripped the strands, and jerked her head back. He angled his head, opened his mouth wider, silently demanding she give him more. Moaning, she rose on the tips of her toes, offered her tongue, and he curled his around hers, licking, sucking. He devoured her as if he were a starving man with an endless feast laid out before him.

"Not enough," he muttered, scattering hard kisses across her cheek and chin. He nipped at her jaw, easing the slight stings with tender brushes of his lips. She didn't want to be eased—she wanted his bites, his almost bruising grip, his wild passion. So she sank her teeth into his bottom lip, suckled hard. Shane growled, and she swallowed the dark sound as if it were the sweetest wine. "Fallon," he warned, the low rumble in his voice ominous...sexy as hell.

"Don't handle me," she rasped, repeating her earlier admonishment. "I want to be fucked, not fondled."

His precious, much-lauded control snapped. She saw the instant it cracked like a twig. Heat like dry lightning crackled in his bright gaze, and the skin across his sharp cheekbones tautened. In contrast, the erotic curves of his mouth, damp from their kiss, seemed more lush, more sensual. Before she could draw her next breath, he gripped the hem of her sweater and ripped it over her head, leaving her standing half-naked in a silk-and-lace bra and jeans.

A hard, demanding hand tangled in her hair, dragging her head back until the tendons protested with a faint throb. "I'll fuck you, baby. I'll give you everything you need and want. But just for however long we're here. No strings, no regrets. You understand?" He crushed his mouth to hers. "Tell me you understand, baby. Say yes."

"Yes." Anything he wanted. Just as long as he didn't stop touching her. She reached for him, but he knocked her hands aside, and lowering his head, latched onto her nipple over light blue silk.

"Oh God, Shane." She panted. So much pleasure. So much. She sucked in another tight breath, grabbed his head, and cradled him to her. Or tried to push him away. Damn, she wasn't sure. His tongue swirled around her nipple, stroked, sucked, even as he plucked at the other rigid tip. Every pinch resonated in her clit, leaving the tiny bundle of nerves quivering and spasming. Liquid heat pooled in her sex, dampened the swollen folds and her panties. Her core contracted, desperate to have any part of him—fingers, tongue, cock—fill her, to ease the empty ache. With one last delicious lick, he switched his attention to her neglected breast. He yanked her bra strap down her shoulder and tugged the cup under her sensitive flesh. Warm air washed over her skin seconds before he cupped the underside of the heavy mound and raked his teeth over the nipple before drawing her into his hot, wicked mouth. She whispered his name again, digging her nails into scalp.

His mouth seared her, right past skin, tissue, and bone to her soul. Each lash of his tongue, each hard suckle of his lips tugged on her heart, reopening a door she'd sealed shut long ago. His touch—God, if she were smart, she'd end this now. Push him away before one more caress, one more moan embedded themselves so deep in her psyche, she would never be able to remove him.

Now. Do it now before it's too late, the last vestiges of sanity hissed. But as he released her nipple with a soft pop and skimmed down over her belly, licking a path above the waistband of her jeans, she ignored the warning. Yeah, she might—would most likely—be hurt and nursing a beaten-to-hell-and-back heart after this, but to have him for whatever amount of time they had available? The pain would be worth the memories she'd create in the here and now. To hell with the consequences. She'd deal with them later.

She smoothed her palms over his short, surprisingly soft hair, down his lean cheeks, and over his strong jaw. Bristles heralding the beginning of a five o'clock shadow scraped her skin, and she shivered, tucking the detail away in the growing sensory file she'd pore over later when remembering this moment. She started to sink to the floor, needing to join him, but he surged upward, took her mouth in a burning kiss. God, the man knew how to make love with his lips and tongue. And still she longed for—craved—more.

As if he'd overheard her silent plea, he cupped her ass and hiked her in his arms. Not needing instructions, she wrapped her thighs around his hips, locking her ankles at the small of his back. The position opened her wide, pressed his cock against her clit. Unable to help herself, she circled her hips, grinding her pussy over his erection. Pleasure blasted through her, a blistering backlash. Whimpering, she did it again. And again. More moisture spilled from between her feminine lips. At this rate, when he got around to removing her jeans, her panties would be soaking wet.

"Fuck, baby," he swore, tightening his grip on her bottom. "I'm trying to walk here, and you're not helping." But he lifted her ass and rotated her sex over his dick in a tight, small circle. Her head dropped back on her shoulders, and he set his teeth over the tendon in her neck, and rolled her over his rigid length once, twice, three more times. *Wait.*

Did she say that aloud? Because if he didn't stop, if he didn't wait… Oh *God*.

She exploded. Orgasm rocked over her, through her, and she shook in his arms.

"Damn, that was hot." His hoarse praise barely reached her past the dull roar in her ears, the cataclysmic wakes in her body. Hard fingers bit into her ass, aided her in maintaining a steady ride when the erotic quakes turned her movements jerky, desperate. "Again. I want that again around my fingers, my tongue, my dick. You're going to give it to me, Fallon."

She nodded…maybe. Jesus, the release had left her muscles as loose as overcooked noodles. He stalked across the room, and when the wide couch cushion hit her back she heaved a sigh of relief. Oh thank *God* he wasn't going to try and He-Man it up the stairs. Even though she'd just come, already the boneless lassitude slowly dissipated, and the encroaching hunger returned, more demanding, more insistent. She raised her arms above her head, hooked her fingers onto the couch arm. His hooded gaze dropped to her chest, brightening with lust.

He rested his hands on her belly, then slid them over her torso, pausing at her breasts to pinch and twist her nipples before continuing up, up, up until his fingers tangled with hers, and his body covered hers like a living, breathing blanket.

Oh. He felt so…*good*.

His weight crushed her, and it was delicious. She closed her eyes, savored his heaviness, how every contour and ridge molded to her curves. Curves she'd always cursed until this moment when they counterbalanced his angles so perfectly. As if they were fashioned for this moment, this purpose. She arched her back, rubbing her nipples back and forth over the soft nub of his sweater.

"Shane," she murmured.

He reared back, freed the button at her waistband. "Shut up, Fallon. No talking unless it's to say 'fuck me' or 'fuck me harder.'"

"Oh." She blinked. "Well in that case," she smiled, "fuck me."

He grunted, tugging her zipper. "I should've known shutting up was off the table," he growled, but a grin twitched the corner of his mouth. Within moments, he had her jeans off, her underwear following seconds later. His big palms widened her thighs, and air brushed over her exposed sex—her exposed, soaking sex. He had a front-seat view of her desire for him while he remained fully clothed, his erection hidden behind his jeans. She wanted him to be as vulnerable as she, place them on equal sexual—and emotional—footing.

She sat up, reaching for the bottom of his sweater. But once again he evaded her.

"You're so wet, baby," he murmured, slipping off the couch and kneeling on the floor. "So damn wet. For me."

Reverence laced his voice as he bent one knee, setting her foot on the cushion, and lifting the other leg over his shoulder. He spread her wide open, trailed a finger through her folds. She flinched as pleasure whipped through her.

"Shh, I got you," he soothed. "I just had you last night, but I'm still hungry."

He dipped his head, retraced the path his finger had forged with his tongue. A broken cry escaped her, and she grappled for and clutched his head, seeking purchase in this chaotic, erotic sea he'd tossed her into without a life jacket.

Electrical currents raced up and down her spine, sizzled in the base as he swept over and around her clit, lapping and sucking the engorged button of flesh. She writhed beneath him, trying to buck him off but alternately clasping his head tight to her pussy. With a hungry rumble, he spread her legs open farther and devoured her, his tongue swirling between her feminine lips before diving into her clasping core. She surrendered to his wicked mouth, the tender but thorough thrusting that shoved her closer and closer to the precipice.

"Christ," he snarled against her entrance. "I can't get enough of you." He plunged into her pussy once more, then returned to her clit, drawing the stiff nub between his lips and applying a strong, relentless suck.

She cried out, hips rolling, body shaking under the lash of pure rapture. "I can't," she begged, head shaking from side to side. "I can't…" Couldn't what? Survive this sensual torture? Take any more of his touch, this devastating pleasure?

Apparently she could, because she cracked right down the middle, ecstasy imploding and scattering her into dozens of pieces.

"Come back to me, baby. We're not through." The rustle of clothes and the muted *thump* of something hitting the table coaxed her eyes open. She noted the brown leather wallet on the glass top, and shifted her attention to Shane. Blue-green fire lit his gaze as he ripped open a condom and quickly sheathed his cock.

She swallowed hard. Son of a bitch, he was *huge*. Two nights ago she'd had him in her hands and mouth, but damn, the size of him still made her belly flutter in excitement and her sex clench in anxiety. The long column of flesh speared from the gap in his jeans, the ruddy, mushroom-shaped cap so large and heavy, it seemed to weigh down the thick stalk. God, he was beautiful. Never in her life had she considered a penis attractive—kind of like how she felt about an avocado. Tasty but not the cutest fruit. But his…she dragged a fingertip up his length, savoring the satin-clothed-in-steel sensation even through the latex. His cock was perfectly formed, strength in flesh, desire in skin. He pushed denim and underwear farther past his hips, and her core quivered in anticipation. High and tight, even his balls were sexy.

Sexy balls? Lust had turned her into a raving nymphomaniac.

He dropped over her, hands gripping the couch arm, one foot planted on the floor, and the other knee depressing the cushion between her legs.

"How long has it been?" Strain tautened the skin over his facial bones, flattened the curves of his mouth. He cupped her cheek, brushed the pad of his thumb over the soft skin under her eye. "I'm on the edge here, baby, and I don't want to hurt you. How long?"

"Since that morning. Three months." Maybe a little longer since Jared and she hadn't been beating headboards against the wall on a daily basis. Especially toward the end of their relationship.

His eyes narrowed. Without breaking their visual connection, he slid his cock between her slick cleft, coating his length in her moisture. His cockhead bumped her clit, and she sank her teeth into her lip, groaning and twisting, silently pleading.

"Ready?" he ground out, lodging the tip at her opening. She nodded, locking her fingers around his wrists. He acknowledged her response with a dip of his chin, then pushed forward. Inch by inch he entered her, withdrawing and thrusting a bit more of his length inside her. Her muscles quivered around his cock, working to accept and accommodate him. She burned, the slight sting of unused tissue blending with the ecstasy of being filled and stretched by him. Unbidden, her hips lifted, offering herself and begging for more of him even as she wondered if she could take more.

His erotic assault on her flesh was tender but relentless. He didn't stop until he was buried deep, so deep within her she almost asked him to pull out. There was so much of him—and not just his size and width. But he was inside her, surrounding her, covering her. At that moment she knew—just *knew*—she would never be rid of him. He'd permanently imprinted himself on her sex, her skin, her body. From this moment forward, she wouldn't be the same.

And even as desire pulsed in her, swirled in her belly, and tingled in her breasts, the knowledge scared the bejeezus out of her.

"Damn it," he gritted out between clenched teeth. "Goddamnit, you feel so good. So tight, hot…" He withdrew, and she cried out at the drag of his dick over sensitive muscles and tissue. Not in pain, though—no pain. Just the most exquisite pleasure imaginable. Slowly, he plunged back in.

Correction.

That was the most exquisite pleasure imaginable.

She'd had sex before—bad sex, good sex, even great sex. But this—he pulled out, drove back in—*this* surpassed anything she'd ever experienced, ever felt. She wasn't even sure this was sex. It was something else. Something amazing.

Something brilliant.

Something…breathtaking.

"You okay, baby?" He passed a hand down her torso, hip, and quivering thigh. "Talk to me, Fallon."

She raised her arms, cradled his face between her palms, and met his blazing blue-green gaze. "Fuck me harder," she ordered, voice hoarse with the cries she'd trapped in her throat as he'd buried himself inside her.

A fierce emotion glittered in his eyes seconds before he leaned back, cupped her ass, and set up a steady, hard ride. His heavy strokes rocked her, jolted her inside and out. A sexual symphony soared in the room: skin smacking skin, the suction of wet flesh releasing and accepting a thrusting cock, piercing cries, and low curses.

She came to their special sonata, splintering and flying before plummeting down into a blissful, beautiful darkness.

• • •

"Will you tell me about this?"

Fallon's soft question whispered across his chest, a feathered caress. But it was the brush of fingers over the scars on his side that caused him to stiffen.

Maybe she sensed his instinctive reaction to jerk away and roll out of the bed. To escape her inquiry and the memories they elicited. She tightened her arm across his lower abdomen and wedged her leg between his thighs, anchoring herself to him. If he moved, he would have to pry her off himself.

And he was just too damn tired to try.

Tired from fighting the overwhelming need for her. Tired from the uncertainty and doubt of the last few days. Tired of avoiding the dark period in his life that had changed him forever.

Pressing his head into the pillow, he fixed his gaze on the exposed beams of the bedroom ceiling. He swallowed, his arm like a lead weight around her shoulders.

"We were on a routine presence patrol through Kandahar. It was just like every other drive through the city. There were four of us in the Humvee. Khalil drove, Trevor rode shotgun, and Marcus was beside me, joking back and forth as we always did. Though I scanned the streets and buildings, my mind was already on the Red Sox-Yankees game back at the rec room. Then we turned down a street. There was nothing out of the ordinary—at first. I think we may have all sensed it at the same time—the empty street, the quiet. The feeling that something was…off. But by then it was too late."

The whistle of a rocket-propelled grenade shot out of a tube. The searing heat of the blast. The *rat-a-tat-tat* of gunfire.

His heart hammered against his sternum as if he were back in that dusty street once more, the odor of cordite burning his nose.

"It was an ambush. In seconds they had our Humvee overturned and had us pinned down. We were surrounded. I'd only managed to crawl from the vehicle when bullets caught me in the side and back. I couldn't move. Couldn't do anything but lay there and bleed out into the dirt."

He squeezed his eyes shut, and for a moment his breathing grew shallow, the oxygen seeming to become trapped between his heart and his lungs. A small hand cupped his face, and he tipped his head down, met the compassion in a soft gray gaze that glowed bright even in the moonlit dark. The tenderness and understanding strengthened him even as it caused a curious tightening in his gut.

"Then Marcus was yelling in my ear, ordering me to fight. Telling me I wouldn't die on him. He dragged me behind the Humvee, out of the line of fire. Later, when I woke in the hospital, I found out he'd saved Khalil's life, too. Right before he took a hit to the neck. He died saving our lives."

"I'm so sorry," she whispered.

"Marcus wanted to be a doctor; it's why he joined the Army, so they would pay his way to college. As I lay in that hospital bed, all I could think about was how the world had been deprived of a brilliant mind. Who knows what he would have eventually accomplished in the field of medicine. The wrong man had died."

Fallon shot up off the bed, straddling him, both her hands cradling his face. Her gentle touch belied the fierceness of her frown and in her voice. "Don't say that," she hissed. "Don't ever say that. The only thing that kept me from storming that ICU regardless of your wishes was the fact that you were alive. That you were still in this world. I'm sorry for Marcus—I really am. But I'm not sorry you're here—"

"Shh." He reached for her, tangled his fingers in her wild curls and drew her down until her face hovered above his. Lifting his head, he brushed a kiss over her lips. "I used to feel that way, baby. After a while, I realized that I dishonored my friend's memory with those thoughts. As you saw, the scars are extensive. And deep. Though the bullets missed my spine by centimeters and nicked a kidney, the damage was significant. And after I healed, the amount of scar tissue limited my muscular movement. I still have back spasms. Since the Army wouldn't allow me to reenlist, I had to find a new purpose for my life, and I found it with GDG. But I still wear Marcus's dog tag to remind myself of the sacrifice. Of why I can't return to that pit I was in."

"He would've been proud of you," she murmured, and the words lodged in his throat, blocking anything he might have said in reply. The pads of her thumbs grazed lips, cheekbones, the skin under his eyes. "I have no doubt he considered your life worth his then, and he would today. You're such a good man. A worthy man."

Shane inhaled a breath, a knot he hadn't been aware of, loosening and unraveling in his chest. For the first time in four years, he felt...lighter. Freed. Maybe it was finally speaking about that night. Maybe it was confronting the pain, fear, and loss.

Or maybe it was the woman above him. The woman he'd trusted with his truth when, other than the debriefing after the ambush, no one else had managed to pry the events out of him.

"Whatever you're thinking," Fallon whispered, linking their fingers together and pressing the backs of his hands to either side of his head. "Don't." She rose off him, notched his semihard cock at her entrance and sank low over him, surrounding his flesh in her soft, damp heat. Biting her lip, her lashes fluttered before lifting and meeting his gaze. "Don't think," she ordered, undulating her hips, riding him. "Just feel. With me."

And he did.

Chapter Fourteen

It felt like three years had passed since Shane had last talked to Tristan face-to-face instead of three days. He drummed his fingers on the steering wheel of the firm's Escalade he'd swapped out in place of the Range Rover. He'd arrived at the police department an hour early to scope out the location and allow his team—Maddox, Ciaran, and Alex, an ex-SEAL sniper, employed with the firm—plenty of time to settle into position. Fifteen minutes remained until eleven o'clock. Plenty of time for his mind to wander to the woman he'd left exhausted, sleeping in his bed.

He'd had sex with Fallon.

Christ on the cross.

His fingers curled around the wheel, the leather squeaking in protest under his stranglehold. Even with his decision to propose the no-strings-attached sexual bargain to Fallon, sex with her had been unexpected, incredible, mind-blowing. When he'd tracked Fallon down in the living room yesterday afternoon, fucking her on the couch for hours on end hadn't been on his agenda. Losing himself in her addictive taste, her sweet scent, and hot, tight flesh hadn't been planned, but damn, once he'd pushed inside the haven of her pussy… Nothing else had mattered. Not his job. Not his reservations.

But now, with miles and hours between them, the truth struck him like a lightning bolt to the chest. He'd been so damn arrogant, so sure of himself. Even after sipping the intoxicating sweetness between her legs, he'd believed he could have her and walk away without a gluttonous craving for more. But one stroke inside her, one bite of her nails in his skin, one scream of his name in his ear, and all his confident assurances went up in a blaze of need, lust, and pleasure. He'd damn near tried to kill himself last night. On the couch, the floor, and later in his bed. He couldn't get enough. Not of her arms around him. Not of her uninhibited, honest response to his touch and raw talk that seemed to rock her desire higher. Not of her body that molded to his so perfectly, she could've been created for him.

How quickly he could become lost in her. How quickly she could swamp him, blind him. Make him compromise the life he'd planned for himself. Make him forget how wrong they were for each other.

A voice crackled in his earpiece at the same time he spotted Tristan emerging from the police station.

"Tris is headed your way," Maddox informed him. "We're tracking him. Watch your six."

"Copy that." He clicked the mute button, then exited the vehicle, halting in front of the bumper. He deliberately shoved all thoughts of Fallon behind a vault in his mind and slammed the door shut. Every bit of his focus had to be on this meeting ahead of him. Still, he mentally ran down the email he received from Rafe this morning. The night before, Shane had told Fallon there was other currency besides money to bribe a man. On a hunch, Shane had Rafe check anything in Tristan's account having to do with Joy, his friend's fiancée.

Jackpot.

Within moments, Tristan approached him. The silence between them was tense, heavy—unnatural. The ugly presence of the uneasiness stirred the embers of anger in his gut. He despised the poisonous seeds of mistrust that shouldn't exist.

"Tristan." He glanced down at his friend's empty hands. "I thought I was supposed to be looking at mug shots and giving a statement."

"What's going on?" Tristan demanded, voice soft but with a vein of underlying steel. The same flint glittered in his gaze. "Ciaran isn't telling me anything. You're not talking. And our agreement was to stay in contact, to work together. But there's more here, isn't there? More than protecting Fallon."

Shane studied his friend's face, searching. They were never ones to mince words with each other, and he didn't intend to start a new trend now.

"The leak of Fallon's identity. How Michaels's gang knew the exact date of his pretrial hearing. The location of my house. You're the common denominator. The first two we can chalk up to police stations leaking like a sieve. But only four people knew Fallon was with me: Ciaran, Maddox, Khalil, and you."

Tristan's eyes blanked in shock, his lips parting. The

color leeched from his face seconds before it poured back in like a flood, carrying fury with it. "You actually believe I would set you up to be killed? For Fallon to be murdered? I love you like a brother, but right now I'm trying not to beat the shit out of your sorry ass."

Shane remained quiet in the face of Tristan's rage. It sickened him to suspect his friend, but with Fallon's life at stake he couldn't afford to willingly wear blinders. Not even for a decades-long friendship.

"Ray Alturo."

"What?" Tristan snapped. "The jeweler?"

"Yes, the jeweler." Shane crossed his arms, studying Tristan's face with a narrowed gaze. "A year ago, you bought a ten-thousand-dollar wedding ring from him. One, that is a lot of money to spend, especially on a cop's salary. And two, Ray Alturo is suspected of laundering money for the Lords of War drug trafficking. Why are you having any dealings with an associate of the man who is trying to kill Fallon?"

Something flickered across Tristan's face. Surprise. Uncertainty... Guilt?

"Joy saw a ring there she really loved, and I bought it for her. Nothing more than that," he explained, his voice wooden, flat.

"And the fifteen-thousand down payment on the three bedroom, South End row house last month? More mysterious money you're throwing around. Can you explain where it's coming from?"

"You've been investigating me?" Tristan demanded, the emotion brightening his green eyes unmistakable: rage. "Are you serious?"

Shane nodded. "Dead serious," he said grimly. "Now tell

me how a Boston detective can afford to shell out twenty-five thousand dollars in a year when that's nearly a quarter of what you make in a year."

A muscle ticked along Tristan's tightly clenched jaw. "I could, but it's none of your business. And would it make a difference? It seems you've already made up your mind that I'm on the take."

"If I'd already decided you betrayed her and me, I wouldn't be here." But the relief and certainty that his friend was innocent and above suspicion was absent. The nauseous knot in his stomach had tautened until it twisted his gut into a mass of doubt, mistrust, and anger. "I came here for answers, but I don't have any. All you've given me are half-ass explanations that you wouldn't accept from a suspect you were interviewing."

"So I'm a suspect now?" Tristan sneered. He scrubbed a hand over the back of his neck, loosing a harsh crack of laughter. "Of what? Having extra money? That wouldn't convict anyone either."

"No," Shane agreed, lowering his arms and advancing on Tristan until only inches separated them. "But add the release of Fallon's identity—the case you're lead detective on—Michaels's escape, and the attack on my house—a location that you were one of only four people who were aware of Fallon being there—and it makes credible circumstantial evidence."

Tristan shook his head. "I didn't—"

A loud squeal of tires cut off Tristan's statement.

"Incoming!" Maddox barked in Shane's earpiece. "Get down!"

He didn't hesitate; Shane dove for the ground, grabbing

Tristan and dragging his friend down with him.

"What the hell?" Shane growled. "Who did you tell we were meeting today?"

"No one," Tristan barked. "I didn't have anything to do with this."

A series of *pings* thudded against the Escalade's hood, and the windshield shattered above them, shards of glass raining down on top of their heads and backs.

"Shit!" Shane withdrew his gun from its shoulder holster. A swift glance revealed Tristan had done the same. "Report," he snapped at the same time Tristan removed his radio from his belt clip and yelled, "Shots fired!"

"Four total." Alex's calm tone reverberated in his ear. From his position on the roof of a nearby building, the sniper had an eagle-eye view of the parking lot. "One on your left. One at your six. And two on your right." A beat later and Alex amended, "One on your right now."

Hell yeah. The ex-SEAL had evened the odds.

Envisioning where his men were positioned, he pressed the earpiece again. "Maddox, you got the one on my right. Ciaran, the left is yours. I'm circling around to take the one at my rear."

"Copy that," his friends rapped out simultaneously.

"And Alex?" Shane gestured to Tristan, flagging his intention to round the vehicle and for him to meet him at the back of the SUV.

"I got your six," the sniper confirmed.

Keeping the line open, he nodded at Tristan, who returned the gesture. As one they pushed off the ground and, keeping low, darted around the vehicle. Gunfire erupted around them, momentarily transporting him back to the war zone he'd left years earlier. But he gritted his teeth, and in seconds, he crouched next to Tristan, their backs pressed to the bumper, shoulder to shoulder, guns raised. Though he harbored doubts about Tristan's involvement with Jonah Michaels and the Lords of War, a part of him stubbornly trusted his friend to not put a bullet in his back. Throwing up a prayer that he wouldn't come to regret the decision, Shane pointed his fingers straight ahead.

"Cover me," Shane ordered.

"10-4."

Tristan shot to his feet, returned the fire aimed in their direction, and with Alex guiding him, Shane launched across an empty parking space and flattened against the side of the bordering car. Moments later, Tristan followed. Once more he jumped up, popped off several shots while Shane gained more ground toward his target. They repeated the coordinated advance until they silently came up behind the asshole hunkered down behind a sedan. Every time he tried to stand and peer over the front of the car, a shot would ring out, hitting the hood and sending him back down again. Shane smiled, the movement taut, grim. Alex was good.

Holstering his gun, he crept forward. The bastard never heard him.

Shane snaked an arm around the thug's neck, his other hand gripping his wrist to lock the motherfucker high and tight against Shane's forearm. Frantic, the gang member dropped his gun and clawed at Shane. But he held on, relentless until the other man slumped against him. Only then did he loosen his hold, allowing the other man to drop to the ground. Hard.

In that instant, an eerie quiet descended over the parking

lot. The gunfire that had been so deafening, ceased. Even the shouts pouring from the police station seemed to reach him from a narrow tunnel stuffed with wool.

"He dead?" Tristan asked, staring down at the unconscious male at Shane's feet as he replaced his weapon in his shoulder holster.

"No." Not that the urge hadn't been riding him hard. "Knocked out."

Shane glanced up, stared silently at Tristan. The detective had assured Shane he hadn't informed anyone of their meeting this morning. No way had Shane been followed to the police station. So that left Tristan. Either the gang members had followed Tristan to work and sat on him in case something—or someone—turned up. Or...

Or Tristan had lied to him, hadn't expected Shane to attend the meeting with backup. And if that was the case, the "timely" arrival of the Lords of War meant one thing...

Tristan might have set Shane up to die today.

• • •

"Shouldn't he have been back by now?" Fallon questioned the quiet stranger who reminded her of a sexy desert sheik. Khalil—his name as unique as his eagle eyes—lifted his attention from his iPad and studied her from his seat on the living room couch. She rose from the glass table, her chair screeching in protest over the hardwood floor. For hours she'd tried to concentrate on the business proposal she planned to submit to the bank once all *this* was over. But with each painfully slow circuit of the short hand on the ornate, gilded clock on the wall, her concentration wavered.

Right now, as five o'clock came and went, so did the last remnants of her focus.

Khalil had been giving her short updates throughout the day. First the shoot-out. *Oh God, a shoot-out*. Her heart still hammered against her sternum at the thought of Shane caught outside, bullets flying. Two in a week. Because of her. Briefly closing her eyes, she squeezed the bridge of her nose, attempting to stem the tears stinging the back of her eyelids. He'd placed his life on the line, had his threatened, because. Of. Her.

Why?

For years they'd been wary strangers, circling one another if they couldn't manage out-and-out avoidance. His obvious reluctance to even breathe the same air as her had never left any doubt about his feelings toward her. But as soon as he'd heard she might be in trouble, he'd ridden to her rescue like the proverbial white knight. His armor might be dented, his horse an intimidating "Man Rover," and he might wield a gun instead of a sword, but she'd never felt safer. Ever.

And her heart had never been in more danger.

Huffing out a breath, she strode out the room and down the hall to the vestibule. For the umpteenth time she peered out the window next to the front door. Shane had been held for questioning, but according to Khalil, had been released about three thirty, almost two hours ago. She scrutinized the driveway, all her focus zeroed in on the spot where the drive intersected with the privacy road. As if all her staring would make his vehicle appear. Where was Criss Angel when you needed—

A gray SUV turned into the driveway.

"He's here!" she shouted, reaching for the doorknob. Joy

soared inside her, filling her chest like an inflated balloon. She didn't question why—was afraid to ask why. And right now, she didn't care. He'd returned to her.

"Hold on." A strong hand covered hers on the handle, and she jumped. Jesus, the man moved like a freaking ninja. She hadn't heard him leave the living room or move behind her. "Let him come up to the door first, and then I'll deactivate the alarm."

The longest moments of her life entailed Shane emerging from the Range Rover and striding up the sidewalk and porch. True to his word, Khalil punched in the alarm code on the mounted security pad and nodded at her. Before Shane could fit his key into the lock, she jerked the door open.

And drank him in.

Grim lines cut into his lean cheeks and bracketed his sensual but stern mouth. His eyes glittered like jewels as they ran over her as thoroughly as she scanned him. Her palms itched with the desperate need to caress his taut shoulders, smooth down his wide chest, and slide over his back. Maybe when she touched him this clawing, empty ache would start to loosen its talons, and she could breathe again without terror straining every inhalation.

"Next time you go off to play Spy vs. Spy, make sure you leave me with someone who speaks more than five words. He's nearly as bad as you."

He didn't reply—not that she gave him a chance.

She launched herself through the door and threw herself against him.

And a breath shuddered from between her lips when his strong arms rose and wrapped around her, holding her close. Only then did she permit the shakes to overtake her.

He could've been killed. And she would've never seen him again. Never have heard his exasperated tone again. Never have kissed his mouth, his skin. Never have welcomed him within her body, moved under him, been broken apart in pleasure by him. Her arms tightened, and she burrowed her face into his chest, pressing her lips to the place where his heart beat.

"I'm glad to see you, too," he murmured against her hair before brushing a kiss across her curls. With an arm still encircling her shoulders, he turned to Khalil, extending a hand to his friend. "Thank you for staying with her. Keeping her safe for me."

The other man nodded, clasping Shane's hand. "Of course." Khalil glanced down and winked, shocking her. "Any time."

As Shane started giving Khalil instructions, she slipped out from under his arm and climbed the stairs to her bedroom. Quietly, she closed the door behind her and slumped against the wood.

Get it together, she ordered her shaking limbs and racing heart. *He's fine. No need to get all emo. He's* fine.

How long she stood there trying to convince herself that the suffocating knot in her chest was due to her concern over his safety and not much, much more, she didn't know. But when she finally exited the room again and headed toward the stairs, she passed by his bedroom. Through the open door, she heard the shower running in the en suite bathroom. She paused, staring at the empty room. Neat as a pin except for the black jeans and shirt he'd been wearing that were strewn across his military-straight bedcovers.

Jerking her attention to the partially closed bathroom

door, she lifted her hand, covering her belly as if the touch could alleviate the widening ache there. A desperation she despised but acknowledged pulsed, transmitting an urgency through her veins she didn't understand but couldn't deny — or resist. She entered the room, her feet carrying her across the floor to the bathroom. Steam seeped out of the cracked door, and she pushed it open. And stepped inside.

The enormous glass shower cubicle hid nothing.

Water poured down over his head, plastering his short, black hair to his scalp. Rivulets streamed over golden, taut skin. And as he lifted his arms to flatten his palms against the tile wall, muscle flexed and relaxed along his shoulders and back, creating a sensuous dance that set up a low, hungry throb between her thighs. Her gaze traveled down his spine, over the dip at the base, and lingered over the tight, firm curves of his perfect ass. And those thighs...

Without removing her gaze from him, she drew her shirt over her head, and quickly shed the rest of her clothes. When she slid the door aside, he lifted his head and glanced over his shoulder. Slowly, he straightened, turning as she closed them inside the humid space together. He didn't speak; he didn't ask her what she was doing or order her out. Instead, he stood as still as a statue, watching her through hooded eyes that were both hot and cold. Blazing with need and shuttered. She shivered. His gaze beckoned her closer and warned her off. Her stomach twisted. Even now, naked physically and emotionally, she feared his rejection. But she wouldn't leave. Wouldn't run.

Picking up the bar of soap and one of the luxuriant bath cloths, she moved closer to him. She lathered up the cloth and rubbed it over his shoulders, down his arms, and then back up to clean his chest and ridged abdomen. Slowly and with dedicated attention to detail, she washed every inch of him, even wrapping his cock in the thick cotton and stroking his flesh until he groaned deep in his throat.

She dropped the cloth to the tiled floor and circled him. Humming in pleasure, she smoothed her palms up his back, loving the strength and power of him. He was a lethal male animal who hunted and fiercely protected those he loved. But who also would allow himself to be petted, stroked. As he did now. And it was a gift, a privilege.

Her gaze dipped to the scars marring his waist and bordering his spine. With his confession from the night before clear in her head, she brushed her fingertips over the puckered skin. Unlike before, he didn't stiffen or jerk away as she pressed her lips to his damaged flesh. He let her reassure herself that he was whole, alive. That he'd returned to her from war and from earlier today.

Tomorrow he might walk away. Tomorrow he might exist in her life in only the most peripheral manner. Tomorrow she might again be reduced to his little sister's best friend.

But in this instant, she comforted herself, trailing her mouth up the valley bisecting his back, in this pocket of time, he was hers to touch, to kiss.

And that was enough.

Chapter Fifteen

"Oh my God." Fallon moaned, tipping her head back on her shoulders. "If you were Rumpelstiltskin, you would have my firstborn child by now. Just as long as you didn't stop."

Shane snorted. "I swear, some of the weirdest shit comes out of your mouth," he drawled, but continued dragging the brush through her damp curls. When Addisyn was younger, he would sit in her bedroom and comb her hair before putting her to bed. But that brotherly duty didn't compare to the cocoon of intimacy surrounding him and Fallon as he perched on the living room couch with her encased between his legs, performing the same task. Especially when she released another of those groans that conjured thoughts of the sounds she uttered when he sank into the tight, welcoming flesh between her thighs. Relieved but hungry. She shuddered, and inside he did the same.

And not just from the silken slide of her heavy strands over his hands and wrists. Or the intimate embrace of his legs hugging her shoulders and torso. Or the provocative scent of her freshly washed skin as she leaned back against him. Yeah, all of those lit the desire curling in his gut and winding through his veins. But they didn't make him shake. Make him clench his fingers in the wild delight of her hair. Make his chest tighten like a vise compressed his sternum.

The memory of her stepping into the shower with him assumed that blame. The gentle, attentive way she'd washed him in the shower. The tender brush of her lips over his scars. Those gripped him like a pit bull's jaws and refused to let go.

"Thank you," Fallon murmured, breaking into his memories.

"For?"

"This." She fluttered her fingers toward her hair. "No one's brushed my hair for me since I was a little girl. It's…nice."

He gathered her curls away from her forehead, then threaded the thick strands through his fingers. The cinnamon-and-gold spirals wrapped around his skin, and he resisted the urge to burrow his hands in them, tug her head back, and capture her mouth with his.

"It's not completely selfless." He snorted. "I've had a thing for your hair for years."

She stiffened under his hands. "What?"

He huffed out a laugh, lifting a thick lock. "Yeah, I think I may have developed a fetish. Golden, wild, free. You," he admitted with a wealth of reluctance. Still, he surrendered to his need and tangled his fingers in the mass. "Your hair is gorgeous and reminds me of you."

He detected her swift, soft intake of breath and frowned.

"What's wrong?" he asked, tilting her head to the side.

Chagrin and a confusing flash of sadness raced across

her face before disappearing behind a mask he was unaccustomed to spying on her expressive, revealing face.

Her lashes lowered, further hiding herself from him.

"When I was eight, Rachel Bowers told me I had 'nappy' hair. Up until then I'd never questioned why I had tight curls and both my parents had bone-straight hair, but suddenly, thanks to that little bitch, I did. Even though I was a kid, some sense of self-preservation kept me from asking my mother why. It didn't matter though, because a year later I overheard my parents arguing, and my mother yelled at my father that I wasn't his daughter." Shane's hand tightened as he went rigid behind her. "At nine, my rose-colored glasses had been ripped off. Suddenly, I understood why I was so different from the people I'd called Mom and Dad. Why my skin was a couple of shades darker than theirs. Why I had gray eyes when my mother's were green and my father's were brown. Why I was short and thick while my parents were both tall and slender."

"Fallon." Shane breathed. He cupped her chin, tried to turn her more fully toward him, but she resisted.

"Dad never treated me different. Even after he and Mom divorced, he never brought up the fact that I may not be his biological child. Still, I couldn't help—*can't* help— believe every time he sees me…my hair, my skin, my appearance…he's reminded of the possibility, of my mother's betrayal and lies. And I can't help but wonder if that's why he's so cold and distant. I've never mustered up the courage to ask him or Mom. Partly because I don't want to hear him confirm my suspicions. I don't think I could stand it."

"Baby." His grip on her chin firmed, and this time he wouldn't allow her to deny him. He cupped her shoulders and shifted her body around until she had no choice but to give him her attention, to lift her stormy gaze to his. "I'm sorry you were hurt by the adults who were supposed to protect you. And I'm sorry you've had to doubt your identity all these years. I can't imagine how painful the uncertainty has been for you. But everything you've mentioned—every difference you've listed—they're what make you beautiful."

He lifted a strand off her shoulder, held the curl up, and studied it in the waning late afternoon light as dusk crept across the sky. After a moment, he released the lock and trailed his hand over her shoulder and down her arm.

"They make you unique," he murmured, studying the difference between the shades of their flesh. "Your skin reminds me of honey and cinnamon. And for years I've obsessed about your taste, driving myself insane wondering if you would be as sweet on my tongue." His burning gaze flashed upward, crashed into hers. "You are."

She blinked, again lowered her lashes but not before he caught the moisture glistening in her eyes. Her teeth sank into her lower lip, and he gently tugged it free, grazing his thumb across the abused flesh. Uttering her name, he tugged her to her knees and pulled her into his arms, her legs straddling his legs, her head tucked under his chin. He pressed a kiss to her hair, the sight of this unbreakable woman so vulnerable tearing a gaping hole in his chest.

She lifted her hand to his face, and he stared into the desire deepening her dove-gray eyes. A slow, thick heat sidled through his veins. He'd become well acquainted with that particular shade in the past week—it was the same shade when she'd crossed the floor of his bedroom before taking him deep into her mouth. The same shade when he kissed her. The same shade when he first penetrated her pussy with his cock.

Yeah, well acquainted with that look. And he'd come to crave it.

Tilting his head down, Fallon studied him for several long moments. What did she see? Most likely something he was terrified of her noticing, but it couldn't be helped. The shield he'd erected between them years ago wore so many fissures, they resembled spider veins. At one time he'd managed to maintain the facade of polite distance, had cemented the pretense of indifference. But now, after several days with her, rebuilding the wall seemed not only impossible but futile.

"It seems for the past three months I've known nothing but fear. And now I'm shut up in a safe house, the murderer I'm set to testify against probably looking for me at this very moment. And yet," she murmured, tracing the lines of his mouth with a fingertip. "And yet, these past few days have been the happiest of my life. Thank you, Shane. Thank you for coming for me, for protecting me, for giving me new memories. No matter what happens after we leave here, I'll never forget them."

Then her mouth was on his, drowning out the unease slicing through his chest at her fatalistic tone. Her tongue teased the seam of his lips before demanding entrance — which he conceded. With a hungry growl, he allowed her in and yanked away control of the kiss. Gripping her waist, he lifted her up and dragged her over his lap so she straddled his thighs. He tugged her closer until her lovely breasts were crushed to his chest, her pussy in perfect alignment with his dick. He rocked against her and swallowed the low moan she released. Her hands abandoned his face, and she wrapped her arms around his neck, opening wider under his tongue. He suckled, licked, and consumed, unable to get enough of her even as he took...even as a small part of him acknowledged he'd never be able to get enough of her.

She nipped his bottom lip, raked his chin and neck with her teeth. Clenching his jaw, he tipped his head back, granting her easier access. His fingers tightened on her ass, and he ground harder against her, the primal caress of her teeth on skin arrowing straight to his balls. And when she drew his flesh into her mouth and sucked, his cock jerked in jealousy. He stroked his palms up her spine and into her hair, pressing her close, silently ordering her to continue the delicious pressure. Christ, he could imagine the same action around the head of his dick. Could feel the same suction taking him deeper and deeper into that beautiful, wicked mouth.

Eager fingers gripped the hem of his sweater and jerked the knit up his torso. Obediently, he raised his arms, and she tugged the material off.

"God, you're beautiful." Her soft sigh whispered across his skin as she sidled off his lap and knelt on the floor between his thighs. Her words seemed as reverent as the lips she slid down his abdomen and chest. His heart thumped against his rib cage and under her palms. No one had ever called him beautiful; applying the word to him should've sounded silly falling off her lips. Instead the compliment humbled him. He'd been with women—lots of them—but none of them had made him feel so wanted, so...cherished. "A part of me thinks I'm going to wake up in my bed and all of this will have been a dream. Like a bad episode of *Dallas*." She chuckled breathlessly. "I still can't believe you're letting me touch you, kiss you."

He tangled his hands in her hair. "As much as you want, baby. Take whatever you need from me."

Her gaze lifted to his, and the hunger in the gray depths nearly brought him to his knees.

"I need all of you." He almost didn't catch the quiet, murmured confession. And by the swift catch in her breath and immediate lowering of her thick lashes, he had the impression she might not have meant to utter the telling words aloud. Too late, though. He'd heard. And he wouldn't allow her to retract them or pretend she hadn't voiced them.

"Then take it, Fallon," he growled. "It's yours." *Me*, he silently amended. *Take me.* The primitive need to claim and be claimed roared inside him like a ferocious lion, but a sudden vulnerability prohibited him from stating the telltale declaration at the last moment. *It* was harmless. *It* meant his body, his cock, the pleasure he offered. But *me…me* referred to everything. His body, his heart, his mind, all his faults… his life.

Yeah, *it* was safer.

She lowered her head and opened her mouth over his chest. Her soft, quick tongue flicked his nipple, and he jerked under the erotic lash.

"Damn it." He lowered a hand to her waist, then trailed it back up her torso and under her sweater until he cupped a breast. "Harder, Fallon," he rasped, demanded.

With a slightly strangled moan, she closed her lips over his nipple and worried the pebbled tip with her teeth. His hips bucked at the edge of pain mixed with gut-twisting pleasure. He loved that, craved it again, and told her so. As she repeated the caress, he tugged the cups of her bra down and grazed the taut beads with his thumbs. She cried out against his flesh, her fingers digging into his waist. He circled and pinched the peaks, and she reciprocated with hard, pointed stabs of her tongue to his nipples. Every lap and nibble strung him tighter than a quivering guitar string. Her lips and tongue played him as skillfully as any musician.

Panting, she shoved away from him and peeled her sweater off. All those gorgeous honey-and-chocolate curls bounced around her face and shoulders, and an erotic shiver tripped down his spine.

"Come here," he murmured, reaching for her, but she plucked his fingers and, with a smile that would've done a siren proud, slowly released the button on his jeans, lowered the zipper.

"I'm taking what's mine," she reminded him. "You promised."

"Wait, wait." His heart thumped like an eternally late white rabbit. He whipped his discarded sweater up from the cushion next to him and, bending over, folded the knit and padded the floor. Straightening again, he paused at her stunned, wide stare. "What?" he asked, cradling her head. "What's wrong?"

She blinked. Shook her head. Cleared her throat. "Nothing. I—" A tremulous smile ghosted across her lips. "Nothing," she softly repeated. "Absolutely," she pressed a tender kiss to his abdomen, "nothing." Another kiss brushed the patch of skin about the band of his boxer briefs. He didn't know which one trapped the air in his lungs—the gentleness in the sweet caress or having her mouth so close to his dick.

Air wrapped around the tip of his cock seconds before her lips did.

"Oh fuck." Wet, slick heat. Tight, eye-crossing suction. Her hand fisted the bottom of his shaft, setting up a slow, hard pump while her tongue swirled around and under the rim, hitting a spot that had him almost forgetting his damn name. *Jesus.* She was good. So good he didn't know whether to yell at her for the erotic knowledge or babble his thanks and praises. She engulfed another couple of inches. *Praises. Son of a bitch, definitely praises.*

He groaned, his head falling back on his shoulders, fingers gripping her bright strands. Then, seconds later, he lifted his head and dropped it forward, damned if he missed a moment of her beautiful mouth taking his dick. He withdrew, then deliberately thrust forward, watching his rigid flesh part her full, sensual lips. Stared as her mouth bumped her fist at the midway point of his cock.

"Damn, that's pretty," he whispered. "So pretty. Take your hand away."

Her eyes flicked up to his, and he detected the flash of uncertainty in them before she complied, curling her fingers into the denim covering his thighs. He held her head steady as he slowly fed her his cock until the head bumped the back of her throat. She shifted, gagged, her nails biting him through his jeans.

"Easy, baby," he crooned. "Relax your throat. You can do it." Her muscles loosened, no longer trying to expel him from the slim channel. "God, yes. That's it," he growled, pulling free of her mouth and then returning with a slow thrust along her flattened tongue. Her moist heat covered over half his cock.

Lust and hunger swelled in his chest, rippled down his spine, and sizzled in his balls. She swallowed, and he gritted his teeth to force back the orgasm tingling at the small of his back. *Shit, so close. So damn close.* Surrendering to the need clawing at his insides, he fucked her mouth with short, hard strokes, and the fire of release licked at him, the flames burning higher, the wet sounds of sucking his dick stoking the lust, adding kindling to the need.

"No." Desperation wrenched the denial from him even as he yanked her away and up to her feet. Her eyes were hazy with passion, lips wet and swollen from him riding her mouth. Snarling, he released her button and tore off her jeans and panties. "I want to come in your pussy, not your mouth."

He shot to his feet, hiked her in his arms, and strode to the nearby table, setting her on it. Hurriedly, he removed his wallet and a condom from the fold. In seconds, he had his jeans shoved down his hips, the condom rolled over his cock, and her legs wrapped around his hips. He fisted the base of his erection, pressed the cockhead against her folds, and was captivated as her small opening stretched to accommodate him, accept him, suck him in. God, it was beautiful. Hot as hell and beautiful. As he pressed forward and slowly became enveloped by her tight, quivering flesh, a stunning revelation nailed him in the back of the skull.

He wanted Fallon to welcome him into her heart the same way her pussy welcomed his cock. Wanted her to allow him into her life just as her flesh allowed his dick entrance. Wanted to create something that didn't reflect him or her, but *them*. Just like when he was buried so deep inside her, he couldn't tell where he began and she ended.

"Hold on to me." The order came out hoarser, harsher than he intended. But the dense ball of emotion knotting his chest, as well as the stranglehold her sex had on his erection, had him hovering on a razor's edge of need. She slid her arms around his neck, and he tugged her closer to the table's edge, his hold on her hips keeping her steady.

With a groan, he thrust deep in one long stroke. He waited, his molars probably ground down to the bone with the control he exerted not to withdraw and plunge inside her again. But he remained still as her muscles quivered and spasmed around his cock, adjusting to his penetration. Those moments fluttering around his taut, rigid flesh nearly undid him. Closing his eyes, he dug his fingers into her hips, acknowledging bruises might blot her golden skin later.

Sooner than the previous night, her core relaxed around him. Lowering his head, he took her mouth in a burning kiss even as he pulled free from her wet, tight pussy and drove back in. Oh *damn*, she sucked him in. Liquid heat rushed around him. Her muscular walls rippled over his dick, massaging him even as they squeezed him like a vise. Nothing or no one had ever felt this perfect—this perfectly made for him.

He angled her hips higher, slamming his to hers, fucking her like a man possessed. Consuming her cries, he buried his cock in her over and over, losing himself in her mouth, her arms, and her body. When she stiffened, dropped her head on her shoulders, and erupted with a scream, he followed. Her sex clamped down on his shaft and milked everything from him—his seed, his strength, his sanity.

Panting hard, she fell back on the table, and he covered her, his face buried in the crook of her neck. He couldn't move—didn't want to move. Especially when her arms wrapped around him. Content, he started to drift when she whispered his name.

"Yeah?"

"Do you think," she rasped, "we will ever start out having sex in a bed?"

Chapter Sixteen

Pearly moonbeams streamed through the large bay windows, the glow, unhindered by smog or soaring buildings, almost lighting the bedroom as clearly as the noonday sun. Shane stared out over the cliff and beach, the dark waters of the ocean seeming to meld seamlessly into the vast key. Cool air from the central air-conditioning whispered across his bare shoulders and chest, and the hardwood floor cooled his feet. Behind him, in the big bed with the tousled covers and sheets, warmth and comfort awaited him. Not to mention the beautiful, sexy woman sleeping there. But here, it was the woman—or the jumble of thoughts and emotions she stirred—that had driven him from the bed in the first place. Here, at the window with its view of the calm, smooth as glass waters, he'd hoped to find a sense of calm, some sort of peace to ease the turbulence roiling inside his head and chest.

Not happening.

Memories of the evening—of the past few evenings—scrolled through his head like a movie reel. Amid the attempted murder, explosion, and shoot-outs, he'd made love to the vivacious, confident, impetuous woman he'd known for years. And he'd held and comforted a courageous, driven but insecure and wounded stranger who'd worn Fallon's face all this time. In spite of a mother's selfishness and a father's negligence, Fallon had persevered to stand on her own two feet, to provide and create a life for herself. And she'd done it.

Yeah, the sex had been explosive. But, even more importantly, so had the quiet sharing.

The sex had ripped him open.

But the sharing had ripped him up.

When he'd suggested this "bargain," he'd been so damn confident. So sure he could keep it strictly sex, and then eventually walk away unscathed and definitely unattached.

Now, after having her, after spending these last few days with her, hearing her laugh, seeing her smile, feeling her arms around him, he realized just how much of an arrogant ass he'd been.

Not only was he scathed, but the marks were permanent.

Still, he rubbed a hand over the nape of his neck, nothing had changed. The two of them together remained a disaster waiting to happen. He wanted family, marriage, a home. She wanted nothing to do with any of it. Not that he could blame her with her parents as a sterling example. Trying to compromise on those basic values would stifle her and one day make him grow to resent her.

An insistent buzz from across the room snatched him out of his dark thoughts. Frowning, he strode to the nightstand

and snatched up his cell phone. A voicemail notification blinked up at him as if irritated at being ignored. He swiped his thumb over the screen and pressed the phone to his ear. *Damn. When had a call come in?*

"Shane." A low rumble of impatience. "Where are you?" Tristan's voice barked. "I need to talk to you. *Now*. I don't have time—fuck." The cursing, the frantic, almost panicked edge to his tone… This wasn't Tristan. What the hell was going on? "Listen, I'll hit you back, and I hope to God you answer. Don't contact me on my cell. I don't know if it's being traced. I'm calling you from my office phone, but I'm not going to be here…" Another curse. And then nothing. The message abruptly ended.

"What the hell?" Shane repeated. For a long second, he stared at the cell. Then, retracing his steps to the window, he tapped in a number. Waited. One ring. Two. *C'mon, damnit. Answer.*

"Yeah?" Rafe drawled.

"Hey, it's me. Shane."

"What's up?" his friend asked, all remnants of laziness gone, replaced with a hard and alert edge.

"I need you to trace a cell phone for me." Shane rattled off Tristan's number. "Can you let me know his location?"

"You got it. Hit you back in a few."

The line went dead, and he slid the cell into the front pocket of his jeans. What had Tristan wanted? And why had he sounded so paranoid? Almost…unhinged?

"It's a beautiful view, but somehow I don't think that's what has you standing here in the middle of the night."

He glanced down at Fallon, who stood next to him in one of his T-shirts. Her wild curls appeared almost black in the shadows, the moonlight turning her smooth skin alabaster.

"I didn't mean to wake you," he said in lieu of addressing her comment. But he should've known Fallon wouldn't let it go.

"What was the call about? What's wrong?"

He quickly told her about Tristan's call and his request for Rafe.

"He's trying to find you," she whispered. "Why?"

"I don't know." He paused, studied her face, needing to imprint every soft curve and stubborn angle to memory. "But you remember what I promised you, right?"

She nodded. "You won't let anything or anyone hurt me." Shaking her head, she chuckled, but the sound was devoid of humor, flat. "My timing has always sucked. But this seems about as good as any. Especially," she shrugged, "considering."

She tilted her head back, met his eyes, hers unwavering, steady, and yet incredibly vulnerable. His heart set up a thud against his sternum, and he almost begged her to shut up, to not utter a word. But he was too late.

"I screwed up," she murmured. "Royally."

He frowned, confused. "What are you talking about?"

"Just what I said. I messed up." She fixed her gaze on the beach and water beyond the window, shifting closer to the glass until her toes bumped the window. "Somewhere between 'I just want to be fucked, no strings attached' and your gunfight at the O.K. Corral, I evidently lost my mind... and heart."

Shock stretched its icy fingers through his veins. *What the hell? She couldn't mean...* His gut bottomed out even as his heart set up a thunderous pace. Panic and...and *something* vied for dominance.

"If it's any consolation," she continued, "I entered this 'arrangement' with no expectations beyond pleasure and multiple orgasms. I promised I could walk away with no regrets, and at the time I meant it. Believed it." She inhaled a shuddering breath. "But then I almost lost you—almost lost you before I had you. And it hit me that I couldn't imagine a world that you weren't in somewhere, breathing. Even if that somewhere isn't with me. This world needs an honorable, brave, selfless man like you. *I* need you."

"Fallon," he whispered, but the quick, hard shake of her head stopped him.

"God knows my parents haven't been the most protective. But you've always watched out for me. Cared for me. And when I needed you most, you put your life on the line for me. Time and again. Now, in this *safe house*, I need protection from you. At least my heart does. The same heart I've been so determined to shield, to hold onto so no one else could bruise it. Until you. I guess if I'm honest, it's always been you."

"Fallon," he rasped. "Don't do this."

"Don't do what?" she asked, finally tearing her stare away from the window. Her eyes were dark with the pain he'd tried so damn hard to avoid inflicting. "Tell you I love you?" She laughed, the sound dry, rough. "I considered keeping it to myself, because I knew that if you even suspected my feelings about our 'bargain' had changed, it would be over with quicker than I could blink. But no matter how pitiful it makes me look, it's only fair that you know I love you."

Silence throbbed in the room. The heaviness of it pulsed within him like another heartbeat. Part of him hungered to palm her head, draw her into his chest, hold her close. But the other half, the half that recognized they would only hurt each other, kept his arms chained to his sides.

"Fallon," he murmured, surrendering to the need to touch her. Even if it was a graze of the back of his finger over her temple. "Baby, what you want from me, I can't give it to you."

"Love?" she demanded. "Are you telling me you can't love me? I call bullshit."

His mouth thinned, frustration welling inside him. "Do you want me to lie to you? To tell you we can make it and later have you hate me for not being what you need?"

"No," she countered. "I want the truth. But not just for me, for you, too. What you mean to say is, you have love to give, just not for me. That's reserved for that special woman you're searching for. The one you plan to have that family with in your big house. I hate that nameless, faceless woman you plan on giving your name to. Who will lie in your bed. Be your everything. I hate her with a passion."

"Don't put words in my mouth," he said, shifting closer until her head tipped back in order to maintain connection. "You make it sound like I find you unworthy, and I've never believed that. I've never thought that. You," he cupped the nape of her neck, "you are amazing. Beautiful. Brilliant—"

"Reckless. Fickle. Irresponsible," she concluded, her voice low, intense. "Just like your mother." A small, sad smile flickered over her mouth. "I've known you for twelve years. You can deceive yourself, but not me. I remind you of her. Of the flightiness that ended up in the power being shut off and eviction notices. Of the uncertainty. Of the fear. You're scared that I'm like your mother. You're scared I won't be

dependable, that I won't stick. You're scared to trust me."
Sighing, she stepped back, out of his reach, and in that
moment she appeared defeated. "I can't force you to trust
me, to *see* me. I would stand by you, support you. I *am* the
woman you need. But if you can't—won't—open your eyes
and heart to me, I can't force you. But because I do love you,
I'm willing to let you go."

A roar of denial lodged in his throat. Afraid? His mother.
Fuck that, she was way off with that psychobabble shit. No,
that's not why he couldn't risk getting involved with her past
their self-imposed time limit. They were bad for each other.
They were different. Addy…

His cell vibrated against his thigh. He dug it out of his
pocket in a panic. Anything to stop this conversation, stop
her from saying she loved him again. Because if she did, he
might do something incredibly stupid…

"Rafe," he rasped, not missing the rueful twist of her
lips. "What do you have?"

"I tracked his phone, and it's pinging off a cell tower on
Cape Cod," his friend said without preamble. "I'm guessing
he's on his way to you right now. If he is, he could be there in
anywhere from ten to thirty minutes. I'm calling Ciaran right
now to fill him in. Still, Shane, they're not going to make it
out to there before Tristan reaches you."

"Copy that," Shane growled. "After you call Ciaran,
contact the Eastham police department and ask them to
send backup. No lights or sirens in case Tristan is close."
Shane stalked to the dresser and yanked a shirt free from
the drawer.

"On it. Watch yourself."

"Always. And thanks, Rafe," Shane said, shrugging into

the shirt, but not bothering with the buttons.

"Shut up." Then the line went dead again.

If alarm wasn't racing through his veins, he would've smiled. But he already headed to the nightstand for his weapon. Hurriedly, he strapped on his shoulder holster, and with economic, practiced movements, checked his gun before securing it under his arm. He didn't bother with socks or shoes. Picking up his backup piece, he turned to Fallon, who remained frozen at the window, her eyes wide and dark in the shadowed room.

"Do you know how to use a gun?"

She jerked her head *no*. "He's here?" she asked, the calm in her voice, belying the fine tremor that lightly shook her body.

"He's on his way. I don't know how he found us, but... Come here." She obeyed him, her feet silently skirting over the hardwood until she stood in front of him. His gut twisted as he palmed her face. "I—"

A sonorous *dong* echoed throughout the house.

The doorbell.

Shane jerked his head toward the bedroom door.

Who in the hell could that be? The police couldn't have arrived that quickly.

A pounding on the door, followed by a loud shout of his name, answered his question.

"Stay here," he ordered, already moving toward the bedroom door.

"Not a chance," she scoffed. "I'm coming with you."

"Fallon," he ground out, glaring at the open door as the doorbell pealed again.

"Think about it, Shane," she said. "If it was Jonah

Michaels, would he come up to the front door and ring the bell? Besides, I'm safest with you."

"Fine," he snapped, grabbing her wrist as she strode past him. "But you stay behind me. Understand?"

"Of course."

Cautious, he stole down the hall and steps. At the bottom of the staircase, he paused. Listened. Pointing at the bottom step, he silently demanded Fallon stay put and crept to the window bordering the front door. Before he could peer out, another rap reverberated against the wood.

"Shane," Tristan's voice called out to him. "It's me, Tristan. Open up. Please."

Fallon emitted a tiny, strangled sound from behind him, mirroring the shock ricocheting inside himself. Tristan had obviously been closer than he assumed, than Rafe believed. How had he arrived so fast? Hell, how had he found them? Shane had been careful to ensure he hadn't acquired a tail on the way out of Boston. A dark, insidious thought wormed its way into his mind.

Had Jonah Michaels sent a man he believed Shane trusted out here to do his dirty work?

"Shane, please," Tristan pleaded. "We don't have much time. I have to talk to you."

With another glance at Fallon to remain in place, he removed his gun from the holster. And waited.

"Dammit, Shane, I know you're there. You have to let me in." More thumping on the door.

Then it went silent.

Moments later, the *crunch* of gravel reached them through the door.

Shane edged to the door, his spine flattened to the

wall. With a barely perceptible flip of the blinds, he peeked outside on the porch.

It was empty. And a flicker of brake lights at the end of the drive signaled Tristan had left.

Bullshit.

Whatever Tristan's intentions had been in showing up here, he wouldn't have given up so easily. Not for a second did he think Tristan was gone. Shane didn't trust that apparent retreat for a New York minute. He remained at the door for several more minutes, scanning the driveway and the access road, but didn't spot a vehicle or lone figure creeping back toward the house.

"He left?" she asked.

A biting cold chilled his blood as he returned to Fallon, shifting in front of her.

"I doubt it," he ground out. "He might have changed, but not that much. He's always been the most stubborn man I know."

"But—"

"Hold up." He pressed a finger to his mouth. Froze. Listened.

A faint sound reached his ears. From upstairs. He strained to hear it again, every sense stretched in the direction of the noise he thought he detected.

Damn. He'd heard something. It hadn't been a product of his imagination. But maybe—

Nope. There it was again. Hushed, but there. Like the brush of clothes against a wall.

Or a window being slid open.

The alarm. He shot a glance at the mounted box next to the front door.

"Damn." The red "armed" light was dark. Someone—Tristan—had disabled the alarm system from the outside.

He sidled to the side, maneuvering Fallon so the wall covered her back and he shielded her from the front. Also leaving him with a clear view of the person inching down the dark hallway and approaching the head of the staircase. Moments later, Tristan moved into view, pausing at the top of the steps.

Shane deliberately composed and hardened his features to conceal the surprise that punched him in the gut. In the space of hours, he appeared to have aged years. Harsh lines etched his lean face, emphasizing the dark circles under his flat eyes and bracketing the severe line of his mouth. Shane didn't speak as Tristan descended the steps, just shifted backward, ensuring he remained a barrier between Fallon and the detective.

Suspicion, doubt, anger swirled behind his sternum, but worry churned beneath the mix. As soon as Tristan cleared the bottom step, Shane lifted his SIG. Aimed it.

"Stay right there," he warned. "Or I'll blow you the fuck away. Remove your guns." Shane watched with narrowed eyes as Tristan withdrew a gun from a shoulder holster and a smaller one from his ankle. The detective set both on the floor, and kicked them to the side. The weapons slid several feet away from him. "Now, how did you find us?"

"Joy," Tristan said, choking on his fiancée's name.

"Joy?" Shane frowned, slowly lowering his weapon. "What does she have to do with this?"

"Everything." Tristan coughed a bitter laugh. "I'm sorry, Shane. I'm so sorry." Pain spasmed across his face, twisting his mouth. "The woman I intended to marry, the woman I trusted and loved, is the sister of a killer—Jonah Michaels. I'm a fucking detective and didn't know my fiancée was related to a murdering criminal. They should fire me for goddamn stupidity." He dragged his hands over his head, and Shane didn't remind him to keep his hands up. "Joy and Jonah were separated when they entered the foster care system and lost touch. She eventually took the name of the foster parents she lived with, went to college, graduated at the top of her class, got a job at one of the most prestigious computer software companies in the state—she left the life she came from far behind. But apparently, Jonah never lost track of her. And when he discovered she was dating a police officer, he blackmailed her. Either she gave him the information he needed, or he would have me killed."

Tristan loosed another of those bleak cracks of laughter. "As if I would have traded my life for yours or Fallon's. Joy overheard me talking to you about hiding Fallon at your home, and she relayed the location to her brother. And this evening she hacked your firm's security system—"

"Bullshit," Shane snapped, stunned. Hacked their system? She would have to be fucking brilliant because Rafe had set theirs up. And he was nearly a damn savant when it came to computers.

Tristan nodded. "Yeah, she's capable. Joy is damn good. A couple of years ago she was offered a job with the FBI, but she turned it down." His mouth twisted into a bitter caricature of a smile. "Because of me. The same reason she stole the addresses to your safe houses and passed them on to Jonah. She almost got you and Fallon killed for me. Because she *loved me*."

Jesus. The anguish rolling off Tristan in great waves

seemed real. The agony burning in his green eyes, too deep and authentic. Yet, doubt—the awful doubt—still crept through his head like an intruder that refused to be evicted.

"How did you find out?"

"Something you said this morning. It was Joy who suggested the jeweler. She told me she had connections there. And then I started thinking, what if Joy hadn't 'just arrived' when I was talking to you on the phone that night Fallon was at your home. What if she'd overheard my end of the conversation? Small things, but enough that when she arrived home from work I confronted her, and eventually she confessed everything. But we don't have time, Shane. Jonah Michaels or his gang members should be here any minute to kill you and Fallon."

Rare indecision paralyzed him. Years of friendship and knowing the quality of the man he'd grown up with, Shane wanted to trust him. But...

"Trust yourself, Shane," Fallon murmured from behind him. "I do."

A tight band squeezed his chest like a vise. Did she understand what her belief did to him? For him? Maybe she did.

"Get your weapons." Shane jerked his chin toward the guns. "If Michaels and his crew are on the way, we're going to need them."

For a long moment, Tristan stared at him, a grim gratitude breaking through the pain. Returning his nod, he retrieved his guns, but didn't holster them.

For the third time that evening, Shane's phone buzzed. He withdrew it, glanced down, and then answered. "Ciaran."

"Shane," Ciaran barked, "your location has been

compromised. Michaels has found you."

Shane shot a look at Tristan, and in that instant he realized his trust in his friend had been well founded. "Yeah, we know. Tristan just got here and told us. How long?"

A long beat of silence pulsed down the connection.

"Not sure," Ciaran continued. "After Rafe spoke with you, he headed over to our office. He just confirmed that our system was hacked. It was Joy, Shane," his friend said grimly. "Rafe tracked the IP address, even though she'd routed it through servers on several continents. Damn, the girl's good." Huh. Tristan had been right about Joy's abilities. The average hacker would never have been able to get even close to burning through their firewall encryption. "The trail led back to her computer. She accessed the files containing our safe house locations. The last modified time on the file was 6:05. Depending on how soon she passed the information on to Michaels, and how his people went about narrowing down the safe houses, they could be on your doorstep at any moment."

Six o'clock. If Jonah Michaels had been in Boston when he discovered his and Fallon's whereabouts, then he would've had more than enough time to travel to Eastham. The drive from Boston was only about an hour and forty minutes, give or take ten minutes depending on traffic. But if the hit man had been in another part of the state, the distance might have been longer. *Goddamn*. He scrubbed his hand down his face. Michaels could be anywhere.

"I already called the Eastham police and they're on their way. ETA ten minutes. And we're on our way."

"We'll be ready."

"Shane." Ciaran paused. "Be careful."

"Will do. See you soon."

Shane ended the call, replacing the phone in his pocket.

"Fallon." He turned and smoothed her hair from her face. He cupped her cheek even as urgency screamed through him like a runaway train. His heart twisted, and a corresponding ache knotted his gut. Jesus, she looked so young in his overlarge T-shirt. She maintained her composure, but her flattened mouth, quick breaths, and jerky movements telegraphed her tension and awareness of eminent danger. Still, she didn't cry out or crumble into hysterics. His respect and admiration for her rose when he didn't think it was possible. "Go upstairs back to the bedroom and lock the door. Got it?"

"Shane, no! You could get hurt—"

He cut her off with an adamant shake of his head. "Anyone coming after you would have to get through me first. That was my vow," he said. "I meant that. Nothing is going to happen to you. Or me. But I can't concentrate if I don't know you're safe. So stay there. Okay?"

She inhaled, then released a shaky breath. "Okay."

Shane crushed a hard kiss to her mouth. His tongue plunged deep, marauding, tasting so he would carry her with him. He released her, and after brushing her fingers over his lips, she darted up the stairs.

"We need to hash out a quick plan—" Shane stilled. Cocked his head to the side.

"I heard it, too," Tristan murmured, his voice lower than a whisper.

Scratches at a door. As if someone were trying to pick a lock.

The noise emanated from the first floor and the back of

the house instead of upstairs. Since he'd just watched Fallon disappear up those steps, he couldn't contain the almost soundless release of breath.

Adrenaline shot through his veins. His concern for Fallon bled away, replaced by the ice of determination and training. When Jonah Michaels had come after Fallon, he'd signed his own fucking death certificate. In blood.

He gestured to Tristan, and on silent feet, they stole down the hallway toward the rear of the house. He pressed his back to the wall, his arms extended, pointing the muzzle of the gun toward the floor. Across from him, Tristan mimicked the same stance. The careful creak of the back door inching open echoed like a screech, as if someone were attempting to be careful…sneaky.

Eyes narrowed, he listened and counted. One soft *shush* of a footstep over tile followed by another a second later. Another. And another quickly followed. Two people crept through the room and down the hall toward him and Tristan. Two assailants looking for Fallon to kill her. He shoved the murderous fury underneath the sheet of ice. Couldn't afford to be blinded by rage.

When the first large, dark shadow appeared in the entranceway, Shane swung, his fist clipping the intruder under the chin. The figure went down, and Tristan tackled his partner, who rushed after him. In quick work, they had the two intruders under control. Satisfaction whistled through him as he holstered his gun, and reached for the asshole he'd laid out. Gripping the back of the man's T-shirt, he hauled him to his feet. Young. He couldn't have been older than twenty, though the hatred gleaming in his dark eyes and the marks pocking his face tagged him as much older in life and street experience. If not for the fact he broke into their safe house and was after his woman, Shane might have a little sympathy for the punk.

The harsh cacophony of shattering glass penetrated the hall. *Shit.* It'd come from the direction of the foyer. Pounding on the stairs reached him right before air rushed from his chest on a pained expulsion as a heavy body straddled him. His back seized up, and a hard spasm had him gritting his teeth to trap the harsh roar filling his throat. *Not now. Not fucking now.* Inhaling deeply, he breathed through the aching throb, pushing past the agonized clenching of his muscles.

"The bitch is gonna die, and so are you." One moment of distraction, and the kid grinned down at him, the smile nasty and promising a hurting. He raised his fist, brought it down toward Shane's face, but Shane blocked it at the last moment. The contact of bone meeting bone zipped up his arm and to his shoulder in jarring vibrations. Shane bucked hard, dislodging the youth long enough to scramble to his feet. As the kid charged him, the deafening boom of gunfire ricocheted down the hall.

· · ·

Fallon jumped about five damn feet in the air at the blast. She stared, horrified and frozen, as a fist-sized hole appeared where the doorknob used to be.

Move, damn it!

Obeying the harsh order, she darted behind the huge cherry armoire, the fireplace poker she'd grabbed from the iron set in hand and suspended above her head. Her heart hammered, beating in her chest and creating a riotous din in her ears. And still she heard the door crashing against the wall. And the shrill wolf whistle.

"Where are you, bitch? Come out, come out wherever you are." A mean cackle followed the taunt, a terrifying shiver crawling over her skin. She tightened her grip on the poker. Squeezed her eyes close.

No! Open them! How can you see him if your eyes are closed?

Right, right. Her lashes snapped open, and she stared at the patch of shadowed space in front of her without blinking. She trapped her breath in her lungs, refusing to allow her soft pants to betray her hiding spot. Seconds—minutes, hours—later a shadow emerged, the dull, ugly glint of metal preceding the dark figure.

Now.

She arced the poker down. Hard. An agonized howl rent the air along with the sickening crunch of bone. She gagged, her stomach curdling. The gun clattered to the floor as the huge—freaking ginormous—man whirled toward her, cradling his injured wrist to his chest. His lips curled into a malicious snarl, and his narrowed glare declared five different ways he planned to torture her.

"You're dead, bitch," he roared.

Oh God. Even with his wrist most likely broken, he could hurt her. *Badly.*

She swallowed. And did the only thing a woman in her position could do…

She jabbed him in the balls with the poker.

He screamed, the shriek ripping through the air like an enraged banshee. His large frame dropped like a stone, hands cupping his crotch in a gesture that defined too little too late. She raced for the door, but then screeched to a halt. Stalked back to the whimpering mass on the floor. And whacked him across the shoulders. The whimpering stopped.

"That last 'bitch' was one too many," she snapped.

"Fallon."

She jerked her head up, located Shane in the open doorway. Relief coursed through her, and she propped herself against the footboard.

"Are you okay, baby?"

"Yes," she breathed. "Yes."

His gaze lowered to the still figure at her feet. "What happened to him?"

She pushed off the footboard and hurried across the room. "I gave him a balls-ectomy. Poker-style."

Shane choked, his eyes briefly widening before a small grin tugged the corner of his mouth. Shaking his head, he removed his weapon from his shoulder holster, and extended the other hand toward her. "Come on."

Hand in his, she followed him down the darkened hall and rushed down the staircase.

"The police should be here in minutes. We'll wait for them outside," he threw over his shoulder. Once they reached the first floor, he flipped the cover on the alarm pad down.

An arm shot around her neck and yanked her against a hard, unyielding frame.

"Don't touch that," a smooth voice resounded in her ear. "Not unless you want her brains decorating the wall."

Shane whirled around, his gun raised and pointed at the man with his forearm shackled around her throat. And with a gun pointed at her temple.

Fear, acrid and bright, flooded her mouth, her chest, her belly. She clutched the arm imprisoning her even as she pressed against her captor, trying to evade the muzzle of his evil-looking weapon.

"Let her go, Michaels," Shane ordered, his voice calm, cold, gun steady and unwavering in his two-fisted hold.

Jonah Michaels's chuckle tickled her ear. "I don't think so. I've been searching for her too long. You," he grazed the muzzle over her cheekbone, "Ms. Wayland are pretty difficult to get close to." He kissed her jaw, then pointed the weapon at her head again. "Shane Roarke, I'm guessing? I've already taken care of the detective. Now, put your gun down, or I kill her right in front of you."

The detective. Tristan. *God.* Was he dead?

"Shane," she whispered. "Don't—"

"Quiet," Jonah snapped. "If you had minded your own business, we wouldn't be here. I warned you I would come after you, that I would catch you. If you had listened to me, you and your boyfriend wouldn't be about to die." He tightened his hold across her throat. "Now put that goddamn gun on the floor, or I put a hole in her head right now."

Michaels's finger tensed on the trigger, and she couldn't contain her small cry as she squeezed her eyes closed. *Oh God. I don't want to die.*

"All right," Shane growled. She reopened her eyes to witness him slowly bending down, and lowering to one knee. He placed his gun on the floor, his spread fingers hovering above the metal.

"Very good," Jonah purred. "Wise decision." He shifted the gun, and started to level it toward Shane.

No. No, no, no.

She whipped her head to the side, tucked her chin in the fold of his elbow. And went limp.

"Goddamnit," Jonah barked, scrabbling to maintain balance against her sudden dead weight. A shot rang out, and she screamed, tumbling backward, Jonah's arm still wrapped around her.

"Fallon." Shane's foot appeared in her line of vision as he kicked the gun away from Jonah Michaels's open hand. He kneeled beside her, removed the hit man's arm, and pulled her up. "Are you okay? Baby, answer me."

"Yes, I'm fine," she said. "I'm—" She glanced over her shoulder. Spotted Jonah Michaels's wide-eyed glassy stare and the neat bullet hole in his forehead. "I'm—*holy shit*."

A wave of nausea nailed her, and then nothing.

Chapter Seventeen

"You fainted?" Addisyn snickered. "You shoved a guy's 'nads in the back of his throat with a poker, and then you *fainted*?"

Fallon glared at her best friend as Addy pulled her car to a stop at the curb in front of her house. "You did hear the part where I had a gun held to my head, right? Or the part about the blood and brains on the wall?"

Addy switched off the ignition, then turned to her, eyes opened wide, the very picture of contrite innocence. "Oh, I definitely heard that part." She paused. Grinned. "Then you fainted."

"Oh shaddup," Fallon growled, shoving the passenger side door open.

"I'm just saying." Addy laughed, joining her on the sidewalk. "You went all Billy Bad Ass on the gang member, then passed out. Sarah Connors would be so ashamed."

"Explain to me again why I agreed to the girls' night out

with you?" Fallon sneered.

"Because you love me and have missed me." Smiling, Addy grasped Fallon's hand. "God, I'm glad you're safe. I was so worried."

"Me, too," she confessed, squeezing her friend's fingers. "I don't mind admitting I was scared shitless a few times."

"Sooo," Addy drawled, tugging her in the direction of her home. "Since you're in one piece with no extra breathing holes, does this mean you forgive me for calling Shane?"

Shane. Her stomach clenched at the mention of his name. She hadn't heard from him since he'd dropped her off at her father's Back Bay brownstone three days earlier with orders to stay put. Though Jonah Michaels was dead and several Lords of War gang members were being round- ed up by the police, he didn't deem her apartment safe. So he'd ushered her to her father's home, and without a word regarding when he would return—*if* he would return—he'd left her there.

And she missed him. Ached to look at him, touch him. God, if the emptiness inside her yawned this wide after mere days, it would swallow her whole in weeks or months without him. But after their last conversation, she might as well get used to the feeling.

"Yes, I forgive you." She shrugged. "There's nothing to forgive actually."

"Wait. Hold up." Addy skidded to a halt at the bottom porch step. "I called the man you call the Abominable Tin Man, and there's nothing to—" She gasped, her jaw dropping. "Shut the fucking front door. You're in love with him."

Fallon pinched the bridge of her nose, unable to deny her friend's statement.

"Oh my God." Addy stared at her, mouth hanging open. "What happened in that safe house?"

"I lost my mind, my panties, and my heart," Fallon confessed, dropping her head.

"Eeew." Addy screwed up her face, plugging her ears with her fingers. "T-freaking-M-I. I don't ever want to hear about my brother in connection with your panties again. Not ever."

"Are you," Fallon hesitated, studied her friend's face. "Are you okay with…?"

"Fallon, you've been in love with my blockhead brother for years. Even when you supposedly couldn't stand him, I knew you wanted him. I already consider you my sister. Of course I'm okay with the two of you together."

"Pump your brakes, Addy. I wouldn't go that far." Even uttering the words hurt. Unrequited love was a bitch and a half. "I love him, but," she shrugged, "unfortunately I can't say the sentiment is returned. It's…complicated."

"Complicated?" Addy scowled. "Screw that—"

"Hold that diatribe," she said, holding up a finger. Her friend's fierce and loyal defense meant the world to her, but at the moment, with the hurt of Shane's rejection so fresh, she didn't relish discussing it. "Save it for after the piña coladas."

Grumbling something under her breath that sounded suspiciously like, "stubborn, asshole brother," Addy climbed the porch steps and unlocked the front door.

Sighing, Fallon stepped over the threshold. "Addy, don't—"

"Surprise!"

Son of a bitch! Her heart soared for her throat and lodged there. She lifted her hand to her neck, her eyes wide, as she stared at the living room full of grinning people. A bright banner with "Happy Birthday!" emblazoned on it stretched across the entrance with multicolored balloons and streamers taped to the wall.

A party. A surprise party. A surprise *birthday* party.

"What the hell?" she whispered.

Addy laughed, hugging her close. "Happy birthday, Fallon! Since your last one was so fu—uh, messed up, we're throwing you a party to make up for it."

Eyes burning, she scanned the room full of family and friends. Trudy, Shane and Addy's mom. Ciaran was there, standing toward the back of the room with two tall men she wasn't familiar with. Her father. Her *mother*. Oh God. How…?

In seconds, she was surrounded. Her father wrapped her in his arms, pressing a kiss to her head. Her mother intercepted her next, gushing over her in typical dramatic fashion, but Fallon couldn't dredge up irritation. Not when she was here and not gallivanting around some continent with the current husband of the month. Friends from work, college, and childhood swarmed around her, laughing, embracing her, celebrating her. *Her*. Even as another friend hugged her, she shook her head, the shock slow to wear off. Addy understood Fallon's ambivalence toward birthdays. Yet she'd arranged a party just for her. It was…mind-boggling. And wonderful.

She grinned at Addy, who'd hadn't strayed far from her side. "You did all this?" Fallon rasped, voice thick with love and gratefulness. "You did all this for me?"

With a soft smile, Addy shook her head. "Actually, I was just the person charged with getting you here. Shane did all of this, Fallon."

Dipping her head toward the back of the room, Addy grasped Fallon's shoulders and gently but firmly turned her around. "I'll hold these folks off. Go to him."

As if God recreated the parting of the Red Sea, the crowd separated, revealing Shane leaning against the wall, his turquoise gaze fixed on her.

His presence punched the air from her lungs. Greedily, she studied him. Taking in the fatigue darkening his eyes and the tension that emanated from his big frame, she had to fight not to reach for him and draw him close. Comfort him and ease the strain from around his eyes and mouth. Touch him and ease the stiffness from his body.

But none of that was her right. Not now that they'd returned home. He'd made that clear.

Swallowing past the lump in her throat, she forced her feet forward. Imposing a calm she was far from feeling into her voice, she greeted him with a murmured, "Hey."

Shane's gaze roamed over her, traveling from her head to the tips of her sandals and back up. When it returned to her face, she sucked in a breath at the heat in his hooded stare. Her heart pounded in her chest.

"How're you?"

The low murmur stroked over her skin, stoked the fire inside her belly that was never fully extinguished around him. Clearing her throat, she crossed her arms as if the motion could fend off the love and need he stirred within her.

"I'm good."

The two words echoed between them.

"How's Tristan?" she asked softly. Contrary to Jonah

Michaels's claim to have "taken care of" Tristan, the detective was alive and well. Actually, "well" might be stretching it. He'd been knocked out, but the last time she'd seen him, the paramedics had been treating the cut to the back of his head.

"He's—" Shane paused, his handsome features tightening in a brief spasm of sorrow. "He's dealing. Regardless that he's innocent in all this, he's going to blame himself for Joy's betrayal and carry guilt for everything her actions caused."

She nodded, sadness for Tristan a leaden weight in her chest. "Yes, I imagine he will."

Another lengthy silence fell between them.

"Sooo," she drawled, hesitated. Stared at his shuttered face and mentally shrugged. *What the hell.* "Where've you been?"

A corner of his mouth twitched. "We've been busy working with the Boston PD to track down every Lord of War member who was involved with coming after you. With Jonah Michaels dead, the bull's-eye on your back has been eliminated. We wanted to make sure they got the message."

Relief, strong and powerful, poured through her, shoving away the enormous weight that had settled on her shoulders and in her chest since she'd witnessed the murder months ago.

"It's really over, isn't it?" she rasped.

Shane nodded. "Yes, baby, it really is." Shane straightened, pushing off the wall and moving so close only one of them needed to shift an inch to touch. Yet, he didn't. And she didn't either. "Fallon," he said, her name a harsh, rough whisper. "I was so fucking scared."

She blinked, shock sliding through her like a sheet of ice. Spiders aside, she'd witnessed him face down murderers, had seen him disarm and kill them. She couldn't imagine Shane scared. But as a shudder rippled through his body, she believed.

"What?" She tilted her head back, still not certain she'd heard his words correctly.

"I said, I was so fucking scared," he repeated, his eyes burning down into hers. Branding her heart with their intensity. "When I turned and saw Michaels behind you with a gun to your head. I've never been that damn terrified in my life. I thought," he paused, and a muscle along his jaw pulsed, "I thought I was going to lose you."

"You didn't." She yearned to reach for him, tangle her fingers with his, and comfort him with her touch. But the pain of rejection and uncertainty kept her arms locked around her chest. "You saved my life."

He choked on a chuckle. "No, you helped." He shook his head. "Where did you learn that move anyway?"

"I took self-defense classes a couple of years ago." She grinned, although the smile shook on her lips. "Who knew it actually worked?"

He cracked out a loud bark of laughter. "I'd say it worked, baby."

Baby. He'd called her *baby*.

The endearment shouldn't have shaken her like it did. It was probably a slip of the tongue on his part. But the heart trumped logic every time, and she closed her eyes and lowered her head so he wouldn't glimpse the longing the pet name invoked. Damn, why couldn't he see what he was doing to her? He'd already told her she wasn't the woman for him, that they weren't good for each other. Why was he insisting on—

"I know you're not like my mother," he murmured.

Fallon jerked her head up, not sure which surprised her more: the soft, fervent declaration or the tender grip on her hair. Long fingers stroked over her scalp, cupping her head. She shuddered.

"Yes, you and Trudy may share several qualities—whimsical, caring, impulsive, effervescent—but where she was reckless, you're reliable. Where she was childlike, you're mature. Where she could be flighty, Fallon, I would trust you with my life." He shifted that small increment forward, aligning their bodies. She exhaled at the press of his hard chest to her breasts, his hips to hers, his thighs to hers. Need, relief, and a sense of...security she couldn't explain or contain wound its way through her veins and escaped on a sigh.

And when his other hand rose to cradle her cheek, she turned her face into his palm, placing a kiss of gratitude there.

"For so long I've judged you according to a scared boy's rigid plans and a blind man's inability to see the woman the girl had grown into. To put it bluntly, I've been a self-righteous, critical ass."

She snorted at that. If he expected her to object, he might want to pull up a seat and take a load off. As if he read her mind, a corner of his mouth quirked.

"I know I was the one who insisted on a temporary relationship with no strings, no regrets. And now, here I am, so full of regret, it's eking out of my pores. I want more than 'for now' with you, Fallon. I want it all. And only with you, not the nameless, faceless woman."

Moisture stung her eyes for the second time that night. His words, *Jesus*, they reached inside her, touching and healing every self-doubt, wound, and hurt inflicted.

"Shane." She captured his face between her palms. Part of her acknowledged that the room had gone silent, and most likely each pair of eyes and ears were trained on them. He had to realize it, too. And yet… And yet, after arranging a surprise party to supplant her awful birthday memories with new ones, he—the stoic, reserved, private man—stood unashamed before everyone, declaring he'd been a blind ass.

Was it possible to love him more? Why yes. Yes it was.

He exhaled, rested his forehead against hers. His nose bumped hers; his sweet breath bathed her lips. "I'm so damn in love with you."

A couple of gasps and sighs punctuated the room, but all of her attention remained riveted on him. *I'm so damn in love with you. Holy Mary, Mother of God.* Did he just say that? Did he just say…? "You love me?"

"Yes." He laughed, the sound rough, but light. "I love you so damn much it scares me almost as much as seeing that gun trained on you." He grazed her mouth with a kiss. "I've wanted you from the moment you kissed me in that kitchen, and I've fought it. You are…everything. And I was afraid of making you my everything. Because if you left, I would have nothing." He trailed his lips over her forehead, her eyes, her cheek. "But I don't want to live in fear anymore when I can live with you. I love you, Fallon. With all I am, I love you."

She stared at him, joy eclipsing the shock, crashing over her. After all these years, she'd given up hope of ever hearing those words from him. Even after those last couple of days spent in his arms, she'd never dared to believe he would… love her.

"I love you, too, Shane. So much." Cheers erupted around them, accompanied by sharp whistles and raucous applause. Laughing, she threw her arms around him, squeezed him close, probably strangling him, but unable to let go—she was never letting him go. Growling, she jerked back, glared at him. "You can't take it back. You see what I did to Ball-less back at the house, right? That's a love tap compared to what I'll do to you if you try and take it back."

"God, I love you." He laughed, crushing a kiss to her mouth.

"This calls for cake!" Addy bellowed, and seconds later Trudy emerged from the kitchen balancing a large sheet cake covered in chocolate icing and topped with 2- and 5-shaped candles.

"Are you kidding me?" Emotion—joy, surprise, a bit of sadness, and all-consuming love—clogged her throat, burned her eyes as she glanced at the man she adored beyond reason. "Shane, I—"

"Damn," he murmured, encircling her shoulders with a strong arm. "I can't believe I've found something that finally shuts you up."

She chuckled, the sound waterlogged but delighted. Her fingers fluttered at the base of her throat, and she didn't try to contain the tears spilling over onto her cheeks.

"Happy birthday, baby," he whispered, wiping away an escapee tear. "This is your chance for new memories. Happier memories."

"Shane... Thank you," she said, voice thick. "I—" a slight hesitation, "I—thank you."

He pressed a kiss to her temple. "Blow out your candles, baby."

She nodded and bent over the cake. And paused. Stretched out a hand toward him.

"We'll both do it."

Smiling, he wrapped his fingers around hers, moved next to her, and together they blew out the flames.

Acknowledgments

First, last, and always, I give honor and thanks to God, who has been faithful even when I haven't been. You have blessed me and kept me, and I love You.

To Gary. You have never stopped believing in me and haven't allowed me to stop believing in myself. And to Thing 1 and 2, y'all are my hearts—even when I can relate to animals eating their young…snicker! I love you two, and you and your dad are my reasons for waking up in the morning!

To Landy. Thank you so much for sharing your time and knowledge with me. I've always respected the men and women who have put their lives on the line for our freedom and security, but talking to you and hearing everything you've seen and experienced? All of us are blessed to have soldiers like you protecting us here and overseas.

To Debra Glass. I just love you. You're always selfless with your time and never fail to encourage me. Even when I'm annoyingly neurotic. LOL! Thank you for being my cheerleader, my critique partner, my mentor, and my bestie!

To Jessica Lee. I love you. When I met you in that seminar was one of the best days for me not just as an author, but as a person. I didn't know there was a "friend hole" in my life, but you filled it!

To Tracy Montoya. You're always the hardest for me, because there aren't enough words—or at least I don't have them—to capture all the gratitude and love I have for you. I am truly blessed to have you as my editor and teacher. Because I never fail to learn from you. Without you, none of these books would have been as strong. And I'm so excited to find out what our future books will look like! *hint, hint, nudge, nudge* Well, actually, that wasn't subtle at all… Hee-hee!

To Liz Pelletier and Heather Howland. Thank you for your belief in me and my writing. Your confidence means so much, and I'm proud to be an Entangled author!

And last but not least. A huge thank you to my street team, the Saints and Sinners. Hanging out with you guys is the highlight of my days! Thank you for your laughter, love, and support. You guys ROCK! *fist and hip bump*

About the Author

Naima Simone's love of romance was first stirred by Johanna Lindsey, Sandra Brown, and Linda Howard many years ago. Well, not that many. She is only eighteen…ish. Though her first attempt at a romance novel starring Ralph Tresvant from New Edition never saw the light of day, her love of romance, reading, and writing has endured. Published since 2009, she spends her days—and nights—creating stories of unique men and women who experience the first bites of desire, the dizzying heights of passion, and the tender, healing heat of love.

She is wife to Superman, or his non-Kryptonian, less bulletproof equivalent, and mother to the most awesome kids ever. They all live in perfect, sometimes domestically challenged bliss in the southern United States.

Come visit Naima at www.naimasimone.com.